Royal Christm...

Seattle ...

A very royal Christmas surprise awaits…

As trees go up, snow begins to fall, lights begin to sparkle and gifts are wrapped, the esteemed Seattle General Hospital emergency room team prepares for a festive season they won't soon forget!

Head ER doc Domenico di Rossi has long kept his identity as Crown Prince of Isola Verde a secret, so when his father is admitted to the ER, chaos erupts and unexpected Christmas miracles are set in motion for everyone in the hospital. Now, with lives on the line, secrets to hide, a throne to be claimed, and hearts to win and lose, it's clear that this Christmas will be the most dramatic yet for the team at Seattle General Hospital!

Available now:

Falling for the Secret Prince
by Alison Roberts

Neurosurgeon's Christmas to Remember
by Traci Douglass

And coming soon:

The Bodyguard's Christmas Proposal
by Charlotte Hawkes

The Princess's Christmas Baby
by Louisa George

Dear Reader,

One of the things I've always loved about reading is finding myself caught up in a new world, in the company of memorable characters and page-turning stories. Even now, many decades later, I can step instantly through the back of that wardrobe and feel the chill as I enter Narnia, hear the echoes of cowbells on a mountainside with Heidi or feel the gentle pace of rural life on Prince Edward Island with Anne of Green Gables.

As an author, the backgrounds I choose for my stories are very important. I'm in love with Seattle and its magnificent surroundings—including the Olympic National Park, which plays a key role in both my heroine Emilia's life and in the story itself. One day, I'm going to go and visit, and I might even try to find the exact spot where Dom comes to find Emmy because he needs to persuade her that they are meant to be together. Forever!

I love the setting. I love my characters and I love that there's a little bit of Cinderella in this story.

Oh…and it's nearly Christmas…

Happy sigh…

With love,

Alison

FALLING FOR THE SECRET PRINCE

———

ALISON ROBERTS

HARLEQUIN

**MEDICAL
ROMANCE**

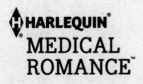

HARLEQUIN®
MEDICAL
ROMANCE™

Recycling programs for this product may not exist in your area.

ISBN-13: 978-1-335-14973-2

Falling for the Secret Prince

Harlequin Enterprises ULC
22 Adelaide St. West, 40th Floor
Toronto, Ontario M5H 4E3, Canada
www.Harlequin.com

Printed in U.S.A.

Alison Roberts is a New Zealander, currently lucky enough to be living in the South of France. She is also lucky enough to write for the Harlequin Medical Romance line. A primary school teacher in a former life, she is now a qualified paramedic. She loves to travel and dance, drink champagne, and spend time with her daughter and her friends.

Books by Alison Roberts

Harlequin Medical Romance

Medics, Sisters, Brides

Awakening the Shy Nurse
Saved by Their Miracle Baby

Rescue Docs

Resisting Her Rescue Doc
Pregnant with Her Best Friend's Baby
Dr. Right for the Single Mom

Hope Children's Hospital

Their Newborn Baby Gift

Twins on Her Doorstep
Melting the Trauma Doc's Heart
Single Dad in Her Stocking
The Paramedic's Unexpected Hero

Visit the Author Profile page
at Harlequin.com for more titles.

CHAPTER ONE

Trauma Team to ER. Stat.

Yes… Dr Emilia Featherstone keyed in the response on her pager that she was available and that she was on her way to the ER and then found an apologetic smile for all the other members of Seattle General Hospital's orthopaedic department, who had gathered in this small lecture theatre to present and discuss current challenging cases.

'Sorry… Gotta go. Trauma team code.'

She wasn't really sorry, of course. Emilia was already pushing open the wide door of the lecture theatre and she would be running by the time she hit the stairs. She loved a trauma team code. She loved the buzz of an ER dealing with an incoming major trauma case and she loved being the surgeon who was the 'go-to' expert for orthopaedic injuries. This was exactly what she'd worked so hard for, ever since those first days at medical school. And here, at Seattle General, was exactly where she wanted to use her expertise— a bustling, state-of-the-art, big-city hospital that attracted the best of the best.

Like she was now.

Like Domenico di Rossi was. As the head of the ER and the trauma team leader, she knew he'd be waiting outside the main resuscitation area to perform a pre-arrival team briefing. He'd have a trauma checklist in his hand, that had items like allocating roles to key personnel, including the airway doctor, circulation nurse and a scribe. He would be ticking off things like appropriate personal protection equipment for each person such as gowns, gloves and goggles and making sure that drugs were drawn up and monitors prepped along with the kind of special equipment that might be needed like a rapid infuser or chest drain. Not that Dom actually needed a clipboard with an attached checklist at all because this was *his* area of expertise and he had always been determined to be the absolute best.

They'd had that ambition in common from

the first time they'd recognised the other as their main competition for the top position in their class at medical school. It had been a bonus to discover that her old rival was working here when Emilia had joined the staff at Seattle General recently. And it had been even more of a bonus to find not only that their respect for each other's abilities was still intact but also that oh, so enjoyable banter that had softened the edges of their competitive relationship seemed to be still very much alive and kicking.

Judging by the gleam in those dark eyes of his, Dom was also sharing Emilia's love of the challenge of a trauma team code. She knew the satisfaction he would have in orchestrating what could turn out to be a complicated response to someone who was critically injured. She suspected there might be another element, whether conscious or not, adding to that satisfaction because, for the moment, he had the advantage over Emilia. This was his space and, as always, he was owning it.

'Out of breath, Emmy?' He kept his voice down so that other members of the team, who were already busy donning their PPE couldn't hear him. 'Have you thought of taking up a fitness programme?'

He was the only person who called her Emmy. It was like a signal that he was tapping into that old banter and he only did it because he'd found it had bothered her so much all those years ago. It had a familiarity that was almost welcome now, however. Maybe because it had been nice to find a familiar face when she'd started working in a new hospital. Or perhaps it was because her past was so far behind her now, it was another lifetime.

'Come to the park with me any day, Dom, and I'll show you who's fitter.'

Lucas Beaufort, another ER doctor, was tying the strings of his gown as he appeared beside Dom.

'Another challenge?' He was grinning. 'Are you two ever going to stop competing with each other?'

Dom just shook his head. 'Lucas—you're on airway, as usual.'

Lucas nodded. 'All set. Equipment list ticked off and drugs drawn up. We're good to go.'

Dom mirrored the single nod. 'Don't forget your lead apron, mate. You too, Emilia.' Dom turned away. 'Where's our radiographer?' he called. 'And has someone put CT on standby in case we need them? What's the ambulance ETA? Okay…let's get everyone into Resus, please…'

Lucas and Emilia shared a glance as they reached for the lead aprons that would protect them when X-rays were taken in Resus. They might not know each other particularly well yet but they were the two people in this hospital who probably knew Domenico di Rossi better than anyone else. Emilia because of their shared years at medical school and Lucas because he was Dom's closest friend. They also had two of the critical roles in this trauma team. The airway was the first step in assessing and stabilising any patient and Lucas would have to deal with any obstruction and perform an intubation if necessary. Emilia would be assessing any injuries that might need surgery and deciding how urgent it was to get someone to Theatre. She was also the team leader support so she could share management with Dom if victim numbers meant that the team would be divided.

'It's an MVA,' Dom informed the medical staff gathered around him moments later.

'Relatively high-speed skid on black ice, apparently, and the vehicle hit a concrete barrier. There are three, maybe four incoming patients and at least one of them is Status One with a compound femoral fracture and haemorrhage. He's unconscious which could be due to blood loss but could also be due to a head injury.'

Dom didn't need to catch Emilia's gaze to warn her that her input into the assessment and treatment of this patient would be a priority. An open fracture of the femur was a serious enough injury for anyone. If it had severed the femoral artery to cause a haemorrhage the blood loss could well be significant enough to not only explain his level of consciousness but also to give the patient an immediately life-threatening designation.

Someone from Neurology was the last person to join the group, just as the double doors that led to the ambulance bay slid open on both sides of the emergency entrance way. With the doors to Resus One folded back it was possible to see the flashing lights of ambulances against the deep grey of a late November morning sky. They could also see the gurneys starting to roll in and the first one clearly held the case that needed the most urgent attention. The patient was still unconscious. Covered in blood. A man hanging on one side of the gurney, who wasn't an ambulance officer was also covered in blood and seemed to be holding a pressure bandage in place on the patient's leg. An older patient, Emilia noted, as the gurney reached the doors of the resus area where the trauma team were waiting to receive the handover.

'This is Roberto Baresi.' The lead paramedic started speaking the moment he was within earshot of the team. 'A seventy-five-year-old male who's just arrived from Europe. His daughter tells us he speaks both Italian and English. He was a back seat passenger in the MVA and he took the brunt of the impact with a concrete barrier wall.'

The gurney was being positioned beside the resus trolley so that the patient could be transferred. As Airway Doctor, it was Lucas's job to oversee the transfer, using a log roll so that the plastic slide could be positioned beneath the elderly man. There was a tourniquet in place, Emilia noted, but it didn't seem to be a hundred percent effective and the face of the man who was trying to keep pressure on the wound was grim enough to suggest that it had already been a battle to control blood loss. Who was he, she wondered, and why had he been given such a critical role in caring for this badly injured man?

'Open femoral fracture and heavy blood loss estimated at two litres, possibly more,' the paramedic continued. 'Patient unconscious with a GCS of seven on arrival. Airway clear and breath sounds equal. Blood pressure was unreadable. He's had two units of saline and currently has a systolic pressure of eighty.'

Still too low. Emilia glanced at the bags of intravenous fluid now being transferred to hooks over the trolley. Lucas had the patient's head tilted back to ensure his airway was open, had transferred his oxygen supply to the overhead outlets and was now listening to his chest with a stethoscope. Other staff were working fast to put monitoring in place for heart rate and rhythm, blood pressure and oxygen levels.

The man who'd been doing the haemorrhage control was being moved aside as a new tourniquet was placed and it was possible to see the extent of the wound on the man's leg which looked serious. The femur—the longest bone in the body—had been broken with enough force to send the ends through tissue and skin, obviously causing damage to important blood vessels on the way.

Emilia's brain was working as rapidly as it always had. She had the ability to pose questions and then instantly provide a list of what needed to be done to get the necessary information. In a matter of only seconds, she was assessing what she could see of the soft tissue and bone damage, wondering what type of fracture she would be dealing with and getting ready to request X-rays of the entire femur, hip and knee. She would prefer a CT scan of the femoral neck as well.

It might be necessary to scan the man's brain before she took him to Theatre, too. The gold standard repair using a rod inside the bone to repair a femoral fracture was contraindicated if the patient had a closed head injury because it was critical to avoid low blood pressure or oxygen levels. If that was the case—and both Lucas and the neurosurgical resident were assessing the man's pupils now—Emilia would have to consider a provisional external fixation for this serious fracture.

More gurneys were in the ER now. A glance over her shoulder showed that one of them had a woman about Emilia's age on it, who had long, curly black hair. She was sitting up and conscious and another man coming in was walking so neither of them were injured seriously enough to mean it would be necessary to disperse members of the trauma team. They probably wouldn't even attract the attention of more than the triage nurse.

Or...perhaps they would.

For the first time since this critically injured patient had been rolled into the resus area, Emilia looked towards Dom. He should be at the foot of the bed, watching and processing everything that was happening, ready to direct the team, locate whatever extra resources were needed and to step in at any time if necessary.

He was at the foot of the bed, all right, but his head was turning from one side to the other, looking, in turn, at both the man on the trolley and the girl on the gurney as if he was observing a slow motion game of tennis. And...something was wrong. So wrong that Emilia could feel the hairs on the back of her neck prickle.

This wasn't the highly skilled and totally focussed team leader that she knew and respected so much. This was a man who was clearly so rattled, for whatever reason, that he was facing a challenge that appeared to be momentarily overwhelming. She knew he was more than capable of pulling himself together well enough to stay on top of the situation but Emilia's heart went out to him because she knew how much he would hate to feel like this, let alone to have any of his colleagues seeing it. Plus, he was pale enough for her to wonder if he was unwell in some way himself.

Emilia didn't hesitate. She could only hope that she had noticed Dom's predicament before anyone else. She stepped close enough to touch his arm and make sure she had his attention.

'I'll take this one, Dom,' she said. 'Go... Take as much time as you need...'

Oddio...

It was every doctor's worst nightmare to have members of their own family brought into an emergency room with potentially life-threatening injuries but, for Dom, it was on a whole next level of complicated.

Nobody could know that this was his family. That this was his father on the resus trolley and it was his sister, Giada, who was on the second gurney. Lucas was the only person at Seattle General who knew why he had such a strained relationship with Roberto but his best friend was the brother Dom had never had and he knew that Lucas wouldn't dream of breaking that confidence. Besides, as the airway doctor, he was totally focussed on stabilising his patient's condition right now. He hadn't looked up so wouldn't have seen, and recognised, Giada and he probably hadn't realised the connection between Dom and Roberto thanks to the difference in surnames.

But Emilia had noticed something odd was going on with the same kind of lightning fast mental reflexes he'd learned to expect from her long ago. Not that she could have the slightest idea of what it was about but her concern for his wellbeing was obvious and Dom could feel a wash of gratitude softening the edges of the shock he was still grappling with.

It could have been enough to allow him to push past the personal connection with these patients. To let him stay where he was and not let it affect his clinical judgement but, beyond where Giada was talking to the triage nurse, Dom could see someone else moving calmly, but swiftly enough to suggest urgency, into the ER. Ayanna Franklin, head of PR for Seattle General. Somehow, she must have already found out who was involved in this accident and she knew she had to safeguard their identities.

No wonder she was looking stressed. It would be a PR disaster if it became known that Seattle General was incapable of protecting the privacy of patients who were depending on it because negative publicity could have wide-ranging and very damaging effects. While a small, Mediterranean kingdom might not be globally well known, the fact that Seattle General currently had both a king and a princess as patients would be deemed more than worthy of intense media attention. Dom had been satisfyingly successful in flying under the radar and avoiding that kind of attention for a long time but he hadn't forgotten how intrusive it could be. Or how far-ranging the effects could be.

Ayanna was speaking quietly to senior nursing staff and Dom needed to know what was being decided. He also needed Ayanna's help to ensure that his father's medical history was available to those that needed to know without revealing his own connection. There were three other patients who'd been brought into his ER at the same time as his father so it was perfectly reasonable for Dom to be seen leaving Resus to check up on them, especially when he had someone as competent as Emilia Featherstone to be the team leader for managing this particular patient. Staff members were stepping back anyway, to allow for the radiographer to get the images needed, so it was easy to keep moving.

Emilia had known what he needed more than he did, apparently, and that was enough time to get his head around what was happening. And to find out why his father was even in the country way before his planned visit in a few weeks' time. Dom needed the sanctuary of his own office so he could make some private phone calls to the palace but he couldn't go there yet. Not until he could be sure that the other people involved were being taken care of, and his younger sister was obviously going to be at the top of that list.

Except that she didn't seem to want his attention. He couldn't even catch her gaze as he walked towards her. The gurney she was on was already being wheeled towards one of the private examination rooms rather than the curtained cubicles that were the usual destination for minor to moderate cases. If that had been something Ayanna had suggested to the staff to protect privacy then Dom approved of the plan. It also meant that he could have a private conversation with her but, as he got close enough to speak to her, she shook her head.

'I'm fine,' she murmured, the assurance definite but so quiet that no one else could hear. 'Just look after Papa and the others. *Go…*'

She was the second woman to tell him to 'go' within the space of only minutes. Emilia had only been worried about his own well-being but Dom knew that Giada would be concerned about so many others. She had devoted her life to being the perfect Princess and their father's closest aide and she would know how devastating it would be to their people to hear what was happening when the family members weren't in a position to offer any personal reassurance.

The other people involved in this accident, his father's driver Giorgio and his bodyguard, Logan were still waiting for triage and perhaps, they would also be given the shelter of more private rooms. Dom wanted to thank Logan for the potentially life-saving treatment he'd provided for Roberto in controlling that haemorrhage but, again, it would have to wait because he couldn't allow other staff members to realise they had a personal connection. Besides, Ayanna was clearly keen to talk to him as soon as possible. He followed her into another private room and closed the door behind them.

'It's okay,' was the first thing Ayanna told him. 'For now, we've got this covered. Nobody knows that the royal family is here. It's still a secret, as originally planned, and all hospital staff are under strict instructions not to talk about their identities, as per the King's demand.'

'Why are they here so early? It's three weeks until his scheduled surgery.'

'I don't know. Perhaps he wanted to settle in and feel comfortable in the place he's going to be recuperating?' Ayanna shook her head. 'At least we already had all the plans in place. I've contacted his neurosurgeon as well. Max Granger?'

Dom's nod was curt. Without revealing his own relationship with the foreign dignitary who'd chosen Seattle General for his medical treatment, Dom had used his connections to secure the interest of one of the best neurosurgeons the world had to offer. It was at least something he could do to help his family, after his father had received that shocking diagnosis of a brain tumour. Suggesting his own hospital for the surgery had been a way to keep the news private for longer. It also meant that Dom could be sure that Roberto would get the best of care.

'He was attending a conference in Vancouver but he's already on his way back. He was very concerned to hear that the King may have a head injury.' Ayanna glanced at her watch. 'I've got to run. I'm going to collect him at the airport and bring him here.'

Stepping out of the private room, Dom's progress towards his office was interrupted by another young woman—one of his ER nurses, this time.

'What's up, Kat?'

'It's one of our patients from the MVA. Giada Baresi.'

'Is there a problem?' Dom was careful to keep his tone as neutral as possible.

'Could be. She's got a bit of bruising from a seatbelt but she's also injured her wrist. It's not an obvious fracture but we'll need an X-ray to be sure and she's refusing to have one.' Kat was frowning. 'And that's not the only thing...'

'Oh?'

'Well...it's strange but she's insisting she'll only see one doctor from the department. Lucas Beaufort?'

This time, Dom simply raised an eyebrow as a response because he needed a moment to process yet another level of complication. He looked across the department to where the doors of Resus One were folded back again. Roberto was obviously stable enough to be moved—probably to have a CT scan, unless he was going straight to Theatre, but in either case, Lucas would be available very soon. Giada knew Lucas because he'd helped to entertain her a few months ago, when she'd arrived for a visit on a weekend when Dom had an obligation to be out of town to deliver a keynote address at a conference. Was this another attempt to protect Dom's own identity because Giada was afraid she might accidentally say something revealing?

He nodded to Kat. 'That's fine,' he told her. 'And, yes, I know it's unusual but this is a special case.'

A special, rather chaotic case right now but his department was working like clockwork and he knew that everyone involved was getting the best of care. Dom wasn't needed and, in all honesty, he would not be at the top of his game with so many things hammering at his brain from so many directions. Even if it was only for a few minutes, he simply had to escape.

He had phone calls to make. Both he and Giada needed to be kept informed, about their father's condition but it had to be done discreetly for everyone's sake. She had Lucas with her now which was a good thing because Dom had a lot to do. Palace officials needed to be informed about the accident and there were undoubtedly plans already in place in case the upcoming surgery didn't turn out to be the success they were all hoping for. Succession plans that were inevitably going to turn Dom's life upside down. He suspected that the reason his father had arrived in Seattle so early had been to ensure that he was going to be ready to do his duty—to his family and to his country. That, even if the surgery was successful enough to give Roberto many more years, it was still time for Dom to return home and become the new King. That the time had finally arrived when he had to give up the career he was so passionate about.

The calm space of his office was a complete contrast to the controlled chaos of a busy ER but it wasn't enough to relieve the tension Dom was under. If anything, as he lifted the phone to make his first international call, it was steadily increasing. Call after call needed to be made. Shocked people had to be spoken to at length and arrangements had to be planned, confirmed and double-checked. It was astonishing how much time it took and how little it was doing to ease the tension. How was his father?

Was he even still alive…?

Fear that he might never be able to speak to

his father again ramped up that tension even further. The need to tell Roberto that, despite the distance Dom had kept for so many years, he still loved his father very much. Guilt was snapping at the heels of that fear as well. If he'd done his royal duty all along instead of insisting on following his dream of becoming a doctor, this accident might never have happened in the first place. He could have lost his sister along with his father if that accident had been any worse and his country would have never forgiven him. He would have never forgiven himself.

With a groan, Dom buried his face in his hands, his elbows on his desk.

Oh...dear Lord...

She should have knocked before opening the door of this office. For a horrified moment, Emilia stared at what seemed to be a more broken version of Domenico Di Rossi than she could have ever imagined.

She ducked backwards just as quietly, pulling the door with her and then knocked on it loudly enough to be a warning. As she opened it again, in response to his call to enter, she knew her instincts had been correct. Dom would have been as horrified as she was to know that she'd seen him like that. He'd dropped his hands from his face now and he was watching the door to see who was coming into his office with an expression that suggested he was ready to deal with anything.

'I was told you wanted an update on Roberto Baresi.' Emilia kept her tone completely professional. 'I didn't realise that he was such a VIP until I came out of Theatre. It's all very hush-hush, though, isn't it?'

'How is he?'

Dom seemed to freeze after his curt query, waiting for her response, and the tension in this office was palpable enough to make Emilia blink. What on earth was going on, here?

'I'm not sure. He's still in Theatre.'

'What?' The frown on Dom's face turned his focus on her into a glare. 'What are you doing down here, then?'

'Because my part in his surgery is completed. We had to rush him to Theatre because he was still losing blood. We got some X-rays but there was no time for a CT scan— of either his leg or his head. We controlled the haemorrhage, repaired the artery and stabilised the fracture but his condition was deteriorating. He's now with a neurosurgeon who was apparently flown in specially to treat him.' Emilia was still astonished by this superstar treatment. 'Right now he's being operated on to deal with a subdural haemorrhage due to his head injury.'

'Oh, no…'

Dom closed his eyes and Emilia could see him dragging in a deep breath as if this news was a body blow of some kind.

'What's going on, Dom?' she asked quietly.

His eyes snapped open. 'Nothing. Why do you ask?'

It was her turn to glare at him. 'Something's being covered up,' she said. 'And, if there's one thing I can't stand, it's dishonesty. I've known you long enough to know that you're lying, Dom, and…and I don't think I deserve that. Do you?'

They'd always been rivals rather than friends but that didn't mean there wasn't a connection between them. A connection that was strong enough to make Emilia want to help Dom. Perhaps she cared about him more than she'd ever realised, in fact?

And maybe he could feel that connection,

too. Because he was shaking his head in response to her query. The shake morphed into a slow nod.

'You deserve to know. Maybe I should have told you a very long time ago.'

'Told me what?'

This was something serious, wasn't it? Something that she was somehow involved in already, if it went back into their shared past? There was a beat of something darker than curiosity for Emilia now. She didn't like secrets. They could be considered a form of lying by omission as far as she was concerned. Dishonesty was more than simply something she disapproved of. It was right up there with not being able to trust someone and she knew, all too well, how that could destroy someone's life.

'I can't talk now.' Dom shook his head. 'There are others who need to know what's happening with Roberto and I need to talk to his surgeon when he comes out of Theatre.'

'That might not be for ages—he's only just gone in. You'll know a lot more about what's happening if you wait a while.' She held his gaze. 'And maybe whatever you think I "deserve" to know is something I should know before I see him again myself.' Surely Dom couldn't miss the hint of anger in her tone—a warning, even—but it was justified as far as Emilia was concerned. If the information that she hadn't been told meant that her patient hadn't received the best care she could possibly provide then Dr. di Rossi was going to find out just how angry she was capable of getting. 'And that will be as soon as Roberto's been admitted to post-operative intensive care so the clock's ticking.'

Quick analysis of a situation and then decision making was more like the man Emilia knew. He barely hesitated.

'Fair enough.' This time, the nod was as curt as the tone. 'But we can't talk here. It's not private enough.' Dom moved swiftly to open the door of his office. 'Come with me.'

CHAPTER TWO

EVEN CLIMBING STAIRS automatically became some kind of competition between Emilia and Dom. They just couldn't help themselves. Emilia had to run to keep up with the way Dom's long legs could easily take two steps at a time and, despite still wearing her theatre scrubs, she was a little out of breath and overheated by the time they reached the top floor of Seattle General. Even so, the idea of going outside onto the roof space seemed ill-advised but Dom was definitely heading for the doors that led to the helipad.

'Are you crazy? It's single figure temperatures out there. The ice from this morning hasn't even melted yet.'

'It's okay.' Dom had already opened the door to let in a blast of freezing air. He was also wearing scrubs but didn't seem at all perturbed. 'Trust me.'

The wind chill factor felt like it was taking the temperature unpleasantly close to zero but, if Dom could handle it, Emilia wasn't about to start whining. She was familiar with this part of the roof space, having been with the trauma team on occasion, meeting critically ill patients coming in by helicopter but Dom was striding past the helipad and around the structures that housed the elevator mechanisms even though they could have provided some shelter from the biting wind.

Emilia wrapped her arms around her body, wondering how far they were going on this vast roof space but then she was totally distracted by the spectacular views she hadn't known were available up here on this side of the roof. In one direction, the dramatic mound of Mount Rainier could be seen, and in another, the distinctive tip of the Space Needle stood out amongst the high-rise buildings of the city centre. The waters of Elliot Bay had tendrils of mist that made the islands look dark and mysterious and beyond them, the impressive range of the Olympic mountains had snow and glacier-capped peaks that were touching the heavy, grey clouds.

The gorgeous landscapes of Seattle had attracted Emilia to work here just as much as the prestigious position she'd won as head of the orthopaedic department in this hospital and, already, the Olympic National Park at the foot of that mountain range had become her favourite place in the world.

A sunrise or sunset from this vantage point would be something to see. Romantic, even, if it wasn't so incredibly cold. Except…to her astonishment, Emilia could now feel the caress of warm air. A few steps more and she was surrounded in the warmth that was coming from the cluster of huge bent funnels that had to be vents for the hospital's central heating system. The noise from the system was enough for the need to raise your voice to be heard by someone standing right next to you which probably guaranteed that nobody else would hear what was said. She found herself giving Dom a surprised glance. Had he come here before to know of such a private place to have a conversation? If so, why? How much did she really know about Domenico di Rossi?

With its usual efficiency, her brain rapidly scrambled to supply the information she had available, the collection of which had begun well over ten years ago, at medical school. With his tall, dark, Mediterranean looks, Dom had been, without doubt, not only the best looking male in her class but with the faint but cute Italian accent to his perfect English she could see that most of the women around her were instantly distracted.

Emilia hadn't been about to let herself be distracted, however. It was nothing short of a miracle that she had this opportunity to follow her dream of becoming a doctor and she owed it to the person who had believed in her and made this possible to make sure she gave it her very best shot. So she'd ignored the handsome Dom, right until the day that his name had appeared above hers at the top of the list of class marks in an anatomy test. Emilia had adjusted her view of Dom at that point. She wasn't going to ignore him now. She was going to rise to the challenge he presented and do whatever it took to stop him beating her again. He couldn't have known the gift of motivation he'd provided but it got her through the tough patches when she was feeling unbearably lonely and out of place so, even though she steadfastly refused to allow any kind of personal relationship with

Dom, and they went their separate ways after medical school, she hadn't been about to forget him, either. She could, in fact, probably remember every test or exam in which he'd scored a higher mark than herself but apart from that, she didn't know very much, did she?

His first words were also about something she knew nothing about.

'Have you ever heard of a country called Isola Verde?' he asked.

She shook her head.

'It means "green island" in Italian. It's an island nation in the Mediterranean. Independent. Has its own government and royal family who can be traced back to sometime in the twelfth century.'

Emilia couldn't think why Dom was telling her this but his expression was deadly serious. This was important. She remembered that the paramedic had said that her patient spoke both Italian and English. So did Dom, for that matter. She refocussed on what he was saying.

'So it's like Monaco? In France?'

'Monaco's a principality, which has a ruler or a prince, rather than a kingdom that has a king or queen, but, yes, there's a similar structure.'

Emilia was getting used to hearing Dom's words through the background noise of the vents. 'And this kingdom of Isola Verde has something to do with Roberto Baresi?'

Dom gave a single nod. 'He's the King. The girl that came in with him is his daughter, Princess Giada.'

Emilia's jaw dropped. 'I was operating on a *king*? And nobody told me?'

Dom's gaze was steady. 'Would it have made any difference to the care you gave him?'

'No, of course not.

'But why is he here? If they're here on a state visit or something, why don't they have some sort of protection team? And media coverage?'

'It's a private visit. Arrangements had been made for him to have surgery away from his own country. There's a new hospital that's just opened in Isola Verde but I think he thought it would be too much pressure for the staff to handle treating their own monarch. Plus, his diagnosis may not be as serious as it seems and he would prefer to reveal it after the surgery has been successful.'

'Surgery for what, exactly?'

'A brain tumour. The expert opinion is that it's not malignant and that surgery should provide a complete cure but we won't know for sure until it's removed and it's in a difficult spot which is why someone as highly respected in the field as Max Granger has been engaged as the surgeon.'

Emilia was starting to put the pieces of the puzzle together. 'So that's why he got flown in so fast. I thought it was a bit over the top for a possible head injury from an accident. The injury could be significant, then, yes?'

'Yes.' Dom's tone was grim. 'It's a bit of a catastrophe really. We'll have to wait and see if it's even possible to go ahead with the original surgery that was scheduled for December.'

'How far away?'

'The fifteenth.'

'I'll have to keep that in mind while we're watching progress on the leg injury.' Focussed again on her patient, Emilia brushed aside the question of how and why Dom knew so much about this.

'Thanks for telling me,' she said. 'I can imagine why it needs to be kept under wraps and I can understand why you couldn't say anything earlier with so many people around in the ER. It's not as if we had time to do a CT of his head when it was paramount to repair that artery in his leg.'

Maybe they were both thinking of that leg wound and how hard it had been to get control of the bleeding.

'Something else you should probably know,' Dom told her, 'is that the man who was doing the haemorrhage control is the King's bodyguard, Logan Connors, who used to be an army doctor. Or *was* the King's bodyguard. He's about to leave that position because he has, coincidentally, landed a job here in the ER. He'll be starting on the first of December.'

'Oh…so that's how you knew who they all were?'

Dom looked uncomfortable now. 'Not exactly.'

That question of how Dom knew so much about this reappeared in Emilia's head because it was obvious that Dom hadn't told her everything. Okay, maybe he'd recognised the bodyguard so he knew who the patient was, but that didn't explain why he'd been rattled enough to seem incapable of taking control.

'How do you know so much about this King?' she asked slowly. 'How did you recognise his daughter the moment they came in?'

She could see Dom's hesitation. The way he took time to swallow as if it was difficult. Significant.

'Because she's my sister.'

'What?' It made no sense.

'Roberto Baresi is our father.'

Emilia actually shook her head. 'But your surname's Di Rossi, not Baresi.'

'I go by my mother's maiden name. I didn't want my background known when I came to study and work in America. I didn't want special treatment or media attention. I wanted to be like everyone else. Like *you*, Emmy… Being able to work hard and achieve my dream of becoming a doctor.'

Emilia's head was spinning. 'Wait… You're telling me that you're the son of a *king*? That would make you a…a *prince*?'

He was holding her gaze again and she could see the absolute honesty in his eyes. 'Yes.'

A single word but one that suddenly opened a gulf between them that was wider than any ocean. He was nothing like her. They were suddenly so far apart that they could have come from different planets. He was a *prince*. Part of a royal family that could be traced back for centuries and she was a girl who hadn't even known who her father was and had had to be taken away from her mother's damaging lifestyle. He was a man who'd always had a privileged lifestyle and a future to look forward to, whereas she'd been a girl who'd been labelled wild enough to get shunted from foster home to foster home, becoming more and more lost until someone— that amazing teacher she'd had in the eleventh grade—had finally believed in her enough to let her dream of a different future.

So she'd been bang on the mark in thinking she didn't know very much about Dom, hadn't she? It was, in fact, so much of an understatement that it should have laughable. But it wasn't. This wasn't remotely funny. Emilia couldn't quite identify the swirl of emotion that she could feel building inside her head—and her heart—but it wasn't pleasant. And it was powerful enough to be preventing any speech right now. Having opened her mouth and then closed it again, she had to give in and wait for the initial shock, or whatever it was that was paralysing her, to wear off.

Emilia looked stunned, as Dom had known she would be but there was more to see in those wide, blue eyes. She looked...*hurt*, dammit—as if he'd delivered a personal blow. Because he had never trusted her enough to share his secret?

But why would he? They'd never been that close. It wasn't that he'd never found her attractive, mind you. Quite the opposite. He'd recognised the potential for not only distraction but destruction as well. He couldn't afford to fall in love with anyone because that might have led to complications that involved publicity and an early end to his career and Dom had no intention of letting that happen.

It had been so much easier to keep any liaisons with women, sexual or otherwise, on a strictly casual basis. And to keep them infrequent and as discreet as possible, of course. It didn't matter that he became labelled as something of a playboy and perennial bachelor because, if it came out later—and it most likely would—it wouldn't be a damaging scandal for the royal house of Isola Verde. He was never unkind, either, and perhaps that intent not to hurt anybody had also been a reason to steer well clear of Emilia Featherstone as anything more than his biggest academic rival.

But had he ended up hurting her anyway? It would appear so, given that she seemed to be struggling to find something to say and the silence was startlingly obvious, even with the background noise of those air vents. Dom was already feeling the weight of guilt today so he might as well add a bit more to the burden but he didn't like this. Not at all. He'd said that she deserved to know the truth. Maybe she deserved something a bit more personal as an explanation?

'I didn't tell you back then,' he said. 'I didn't tell anyone.'

She was just staring at him. Not saying anything. The wind teased a tress of her bright auburn hair out of its clasp but she didn't bother pushing it off her face. Oddly, Dom had to stifle an urge to do that himself.

Instead, he chose to release words that came straight from his heart.

'I wanted a chance to be *me*,' he told Emilia. 'The person I am in here.' His fingers clenched into a fist as he thumped the left side of his chest twice. 'As a man. As the doctor I'd always dreamed of being.'

He took a deep breath, surprising himself by how shaky it felt. 'Not as Crown Prince,' he added, his words gathering more emotion. 'On borrowed time and knowing that one day I was going to have to give up a career that means everything to me and take over ruling a country just because of where I happened to be born. Even if…' He had to suck in another breath. 'Even if it's the last thing I really *want* to do.'

The expression on Emilia's face was changing. A frown line was appearing between her eyes. He might have hoped for her understanding, at least, after that very personal revelation. Sympathy, even. But no. Surprisingly, the way she was looking at him now suggested that she was…angry?

'You lied to me,' she said.

'How?'

'By not telling me the truth.'

'Nobody knew the truth. How long do you think I would have lasted if it had come out? I would have been hounded by the media until I was driven home again. I needed to be safe to achieve what I wanted so much and keeping it a secret was the only way.'

'So you're saying you've never told anyone, in all these years? That no one here knows who you are and that no one from your country knows where you are?'

'Not exactly,' Dom admitted. 'I haven't been home for many years but my sister's been to visit me more than once. And Lucas Beaufort knows... We found we had something in common with...um...some family issues.'

Emilia's breath came out in a dismissive huff. 'Family issues? You have *no* idea what family issues really are. People kept secrets from me all my life and, as far I'm concerned, they're just as bad as outright lies. They damage people. They damage lives.'

Oh, man...she wasn't just angry about this, was she? Emilia was furious.

'You know what?' She didn't wait for a response. 'I don't care that you're a damn prince. I respected you for what I thought you were—as that man and that doctor you wanted so much to be—but not now...' Emilia paused to gulp in a breath. 'I don't respect anybody who lies to me. I *hate* dishonesty...'

She turned away, her arms tightly wrapped around her body. 'Don't worry,' she added, with a bitter note in her voice. 'Your secret is safe. I'm not going to tell anyone about you. I don't even want to talk *to* you, let alone *about* you.'

And, with that, she was gone. A petite, furious figure striding across this vast roof space. Turning the corner to head for the helipad and then back into the warmth and shelter of the hospital buildings. Which was exactly where Dom needed to go. There might be news of his father by now that he could pass on to Giada. He might have just ruined one of his closer professional relationships but he had his family to care for and that had to take priority. And yet, his feet refused to start moving just yet. He looked up at the sullen sky above him as he took several, slow, deep breaths to try and clear his head enough to centre himself.

Part of his brain was reluctant to let go of that last image of Emilia, vanishing behind the tops of the nearest elevators. There was something nagging at him that he couldn't quite pin down. Curiosity, perhaps, about why she was so angry with him. They hadn't known each other well enough for her to be that offended that he'd kept a secret from her, surely? It wasn't as if she'd ever told him anything personal about her own life. And maybe that was what he wanted to think about—that reference to people keeping secrets from her? Damaging her life? He wanted to know more about that. No...it felt like he *needed* to know more about that.

Except that there were other things he had to think about right now that were a lot more pressing. Dom knew it was way past time that he stepped up to do his duty. He'd had a lot longer than he'd hoped for when his father gave him permission to go to an American medical school. He'd hoped to graduate and at least have a few years to practise medicine but he'd had a good ten years to do the job he loved and he'd achieved an expertise and position that had been above any expectations.

And he'd always known that this day would come. That the shackles of his birth right would pull him back to the gilded cage that his childhood had been. He could feel them tightening already as the chains that bound him to his country were being hauled in. Dom was used to pressure. In the early years of his studies it had been to succeed. A wry smile touched his lips as he remembered how, at medical school, that pressure had included trying to beat Emilia Featherstone. The pressure of running a busy ER was something else again but it was something that Dom thrived on. This pressure, however, of facing up to becoming King, felt like a weight that threatened to bury him.

But that couldn't happen.

It wasn't going to happen because Dom knew what was expected of him by people that he loved and he wasn't about to let them down. One of those people was in danger right now and that was where Dom needed to be. He had to protect his father as much as he could. He had to support his little sister who must be extremely anxious at the moment. The driver, Giorgio, no doubt also needed some reassurance from him, even if he had been uninjured, and Logan was about to become a colleague instead of one of his father's employees. Dom had to check to see if there was anything he could be doing to make sure everyone was okay.

He certainly couldn't stay out here on the roof any longer, that was for sure. He felt cold now. And very, very alone…

Emilia did an online search on Isola Verde as soon as she got home. Of course she did. The events of the day had taken on an almost dreamlike quality, despite the reality of her post-operative visit to Roberto Baresi and seeing the discreet security that was now positioned as close as possible to where he was being cared for in the most private space available in the intensive care unit. At least Dom hadn't been there at the same time because she was still furious with him. It might be impossible to avoid seeing him again but she really, really didn't want to talk to him.

And maybe she was searching for details on the island kingdom she'd never heard of because she wanted to justify that anger. To confirm that they came from such totally different worlds it was a relief that she'd avoided any kind of personal relationship. The fact that they were colleagues was extraordinary enough on its own. That they had that competitive bond and were familiar enough with each other for the teasing and, okay, sometimes bordering on insulting banter, to feel completely normal was enough to make Emilia cringe, now. How could he do that? To pretend he was a normal person? To pretend that he was trustworthy when he'd been living a lie the whole time?

He'd said he hadn't been home for many years. Why not? The images and text that Emilia had in front of her told her that he'd been brought up in paradise. The 'green island', surrounded by the astonishing blue water of the Mediterranean Sea, was well named for its fertile land that produced olive oil, tomatoes, lemons and the grapes that were used for award winning wines. The old town, that dated back to the eleventh or twelfth century had narrow, cobbled streets and colourful market places but there was a modern city as well where a new hospital, that the country was obviously very proud of, had been built.

There were gorgeous gardens on the top of a hill in the old city that surrounded a palace built of white stone and marble and the photos that Emilia was staring at suggested that it was always reflecting endless sunshine. The images and impressions were piling up, one on the other. She could almost taste those fat, red tomatoes, and the bright lemons were actually making her mouth water. She could feel the warmth of the sunshine and smell the flowers in those gardens and imagine what it would be like to swim in that blue, silky sea and it felt like Isola Verde was the most perfect place on earth.

The place where Domenico di Rossi had grown up.

No. The place where Domenico *Baresi* was the Crown Prince. Unimaginably wealthy. Unbelievably privileged. And he'd wanted her to feel *sorry* for him? An incredulous huff escaped Emilia's throat and she slammed down the lid of her laptop but, moments later, she was bewildered by the sting behind her eyes that she remembered from long, long ago. Tears were gathering, although they would never be shed because she didn't cry any more.

From fury to feeling so sad? What on earth was this about? Emilia hadn't felt such a rollercoaster of emotion for as long as she could remember. Anger had always been her 'go-to' release for dealing with anything difficult, though, hadn't it? Even when that had got her into so much trouble in the past. Her running away, shouting and breaking things had more than likely been responsible for those endless punishments. For waiting outside those Social Services offices while discussions were taking place about what on earth they were going to do with such a difficult, unruly child.

But it hadn't stopped her hitting back at a world that had promised so much but never delivered. Not until that amazing teacher had somehow recognised her intelligence and had shifted her focus onto studying, along with teaching her that there were ways other than anger to escape something unbearable.

If she'd known there were places on earth like Isola Verde in those days, Emilia might have dreamed of being there. Maybe that was what was making her feel so inexplicably sad now. That longing to be living, or even just visiting, somewhere so perfect felt a lot like that longing to be loved that she'd lived with throughout all those difficult years. And that was something else that made Dom so different from her. He had a family. People who loved him. He had everything, didn't he?

So why was Emilia feeling haunted by that look in his eyes when he'd told her that going back to his own country to be a prince was the last thing he really wanted to do? And why was it, when her anger had faded enough for her to remember that look, she felt that there *was* still a connection between them?

That, maybe, it was even stronger than before?

CHAPTER THREE

STEPPING THROUGH THE automatic doors that linked Seattle General's ER to the rest of the hospital, Emilia found herself catching her breath.

How could everything look the same when nothing *felt* the same?

She could see the doors to the ambulance bay opening and a patient being brought in on a stretcher to where the triage nurse was waiting for them. The central desk had doctors and interns checking results like X-rays and blood tests that were coming through on one of the many computer screens available or standing beside the glass wall where patient locations and conditions were kept up to date, along with which doctor was assigned to the case. Curtains were being opened or whisked shut as medical staff, technicians or even cleaners or security came and went from the cubicles and the folding doors to Resus One were open, just as they had been when Emilia answered the trauma team code only yesterday.

But it felt very different. The head of this ER was not the person she'd thought he was. Instead, he was something so extraordinary it was still almost impossible to wrap her head around it. A crown prince. Royalty. With a background of such privilege that the gulf between them couldn't be any bigger. And that was why it felt so different. Emilia didn't know what to say to Dom any more. She felt awkward. Out of place. *Different*. The feeling was uncomfortably reminiscent of how she'd felt at every new school she'd had to go to or worse, with every new family who'd decided to take on the challenge of fostering her.

Dom was even in almost the same place she'd seen him yesterday morning but it looked as though he was merely scanning the area to make sure it was ready for use when needed. The incoming patient, a teenaged boy in a school uniform who was grinning at something the paramedic was telling him, certainly didn't look as if he was in need of critical care. Emilia didn't need to go near the resus area, either. She wasn't actually required in the ER at all at the moment but she was here and seeing Dom standing alone and not currently caught up in some emergency was exactly what she'd hoped to find.

Because she needed to apologise.

She needed, somehow, to try and make things more like they'd been the day before yesterday. So that she could feel just as excited by the challenge of answering a trauma team call and come into this ER without feeling like her stomach was tied up in knots. She'd been unprofessional yesterday, storming off like the petulant teenager she'd once been and she didn't want that to affect her ability to work with Dom. Was it possible that they could somehow get past this and go back to that easy camaraderie that allowed for a bit of banter?

Swallowing hard as she got close to Resus One, Emilia decided to see if she could take a short cut straight back.

'Hey…' She lowered her voice to a whisper as she half smiled to let Dom know she was teasing him. 'Sorry, but my curtsey's a bit rusty.'

Oh…help… That had gone down like a

lead balloon, hadn't it? Dom's smile was more like a grimace. Then he raised an eyebrow, glancing over Emilia's shoulder to where a technician was coming past, pushing an ECG trolley.

'My office?' His tone was neutral. 'If you've got a moment to spare, that is.' He didn't wait for her response, but turned on his heel and walked off. Emilia followed. This wasn't reminding her so much of a first day at school, any more. It was more like being sent to the headmaster's office to explain yet another instance of her bad behaviour.

But Dom didn't look angry as he shut the office door behind her. He looked as if he hadn't slept all night. Or maybe he hadn't even gone to bed. There were deep creases around his eyes and he might have combed his hair with his fingers judging by its tousled look. And then he sighed and the sound cut through Emilia more than a raised voice might have.

'This is exactly why I didn't tell you,' he said quietly. 'Why I didn't tell anyone. It changes things. It makes it impossible to know whether a relationship is even genuine.'

Yep...he was rubbing his forehead as he

spoke and then he ran his fingers through his hair making it even more rumpled. But Emilia only noticed that in her peripheral vision because she was caught by his eyes as he spoke again.

'And what we had—what we *have*, I should say—that's genuine, isn't it?'

Emilia felt the need to catch her breath again, the way she had when she'd been coming into the ER, but this time, it didn't work. Her breath had already been caught in her chest.

Dom gave his head a tiny shake. 'It's strange because we don't really know that much about each other but I've always thought that you know me better than anyone. Because we're the same, you and me.'

Her breath wasn't caught any more. It escaped through pursed lips in a dismissive huff. 'Yeah…right…' she muttered.

But Dom ignored her. 'In here, we are,' he said softly. He touched the left side of his chest, over his heart, with the same gesture he'd used yesterday when he'd been telling her so passionately that he'd wanted a chance to be the person he truly was.

'We both had the same dream and we were

both driven to be the best. We both give everything we've got—and more—to our careers. To the people who put their trust and their lives into our hands.'

Emilia had to swallow the lump in her throat. It was true. That was the connection. But something else had grown from them becoming such rivals to be the best. Genuine respect. And, while they'd kept their distance personally, there was a familiarity, if not a kind of fondness, even, in the banter they'd always enjoyed. Was that why she'd found herself almost crying, yesterday? Because she'd thought she'd lost that for ever?

'Maybe I didn't explain things very well yesterday,' Dom continued. 'I didn't mean to upset you. I'd like a chance to explain better.'

Emilia shook her head. 'There's no need. I shouldn't have reacted the way I did. That's what I came here for…to apologise.'

'There's no need for that, either, but I'd still like to talk. I want to try and put things right between us and…'

Emilia watched him take a slow breath as he hesitated. This was what she wanted, too, wasn't it? To put things right? Maybe it was going to be possible to push the rewind button, at least enough to let them work together without distraction. Except that Dom seemed to have something he was reluctant to say.

'And…?' she prompted.

'I'd like to know you better,' he said. 'I didn't sleep much last night. I was worried about my father. And my sister.'

'Of course you were. I was happy with Roberto's condition as far as his orthopaedic status is when I saw him earlier today but the brain surgery has to be a concern. Are they going to try waking him up soon?'

'They've already lightened the sedation but he's not showing any signs of waking up. It may take some time.'

'At least he's in the best possible place. And your sister?'

'She tells me she's fine. She's not in the hospital any longer and she's apparently trying to keep a low profile. She wouldn't even tell me where she is. Anyway…' Dom rubbed his forehead again. 'It wasn't just family worries that kept me awake all night. I was thinking about you, as well.'

That startled her. Not that she was about to confess she'd spent quite some time thinking about him, mind you.

'About what you meant when you said I had no idea what "family issues" really are.' Dom caught and held her gaze. 'I want to know what happened to you and why you hate secrets so much. I just…' His breath came out in another sigh. 'I guess I just don't want to lose what we have, Emmy. Something that's real. Something I can trust.'

'But…how can I trust *you*…?'

'You know my secret now.' Dom gaze shifted to the closed door of his office and then back to Emilia. 'You and Lucas are the only people here that know. Even everybody involved in Roberto's scheduled visit and surgery have no idea of my connection to the family. I'm trusting *you*…'

He was. And, oddly, it made Emilia want to cry again and she never cried. She'd decided long ago that she had used up a lifetime supply of tears as a child.

An alarm was sounding beyond the office door and Dom's head swerved, his conversation with Emilia shut down as swiftly as if a switch had been flicked.

'That's the cardiac arrest code…' He was already opening the door and, a moment later, Emilia could hear him issuing terse instructions to get the patient into Resus One. As she walked past the closed doors seconds later, he was calmly asking for someone to charge the defibrillator to two hundred joules. *Stat…*

The cardiac arrest victim who'd been rushed into resus looked barely more than a child.

'How old is he?' Dom was watching the screen of the monitor as he held a bag mask over the boy's face to deliver a breath of oxygen. It was still showing a heart rhythm that would have been rapidly fatal if this arrest hadn't happened somewhere with people trained to support circulation by doing CPR while they used shocks and drugs to try and get a normal rhythm established again.

'Fourteen.' An intern was doing the first two minutes of chest compressions.

'History?'

'He got brought in by ambulance after fainting at school.' It was another ER doctor who answered Dom's query, as she was working to establish an IV line in the patient's arm. 'The paramedic said that the school wasn't aware of any health problems. His mother's been contacted and she's on her way.'

A fainting episode could well have been

a warning sign of the sudden cardiac arrest that had occurred later but Dom didn't have the head space to be considering what might have caused this life-threatening situation. That would come later, when they'd got this boy back.

'I'll have the airway trolley, please. I'm going to intubate.' A flash of thought came and went as Dom realised that Lucas wasn't here to manage the airway component of this resuscitation but that was something else that couldn't be allowed head space yet. 'Draw up some adrenaline, thanks. And amiodarone. Charge the defib again. I'll intubate in the next cycle of compressions.' He gave another two breaths with the bag mask as the defibrillator was charging.

'Okay…stand clear… Shocking now…'

The battle was on and it was one that Dom was absolutely determined to win. He had all the weapons that could be to his advantage—the ability to deliver electrical shocks, access to blood vessels and drugs that could stimulate the heart or deal with arrhythmias, the means to control an airway and breathing, oxygen, trained staff to perform quality chest compressions to keep blood circulating and the knowledge and skills to use all these weapons to whatever degree was needed.

It was the kind of battle that Dom thrived on. It was absolutely gutting if he lost, of course, but on the other side of the coin was where there was no question that someone's life had been saved and that had always been at the heart of why he'd dreamed of becoming a doctor. A success was something the whole team would celebrate—and remember—and, this morning, fifteen minutes after Dom had answered the cardiac arrest code, it looked like that was happening.

'Look…there…we've got sinus rhythm.'

The excitement in the intern's voice made Dom wonder if this might be the first successful resuscitation this young doctor had been a part of. Dom had long ago lost count of how many he'd experienced but, even now, he could share that thrill of seeing the normal spikes tracking across the monitor screen.

'Airway and ventilation are secure,' he told the team. 'I'm going to keep him sedated for now. Let's get a twelve lead ECG. Has Cardiology been paged for a consult?'

'They're on their way. Should arrive soon.'

Someone else arrived first, however. A distraught looking woman who was shown into the resus room, where she rushed towards the trolley.

'Oh, my God… *Jason*…' She reached out to touch his hair but then froze, her gaze fixed on Dom. 'Is he…is he…?'

'He's been very sick,' Dom told her, 'but we've got him back to a normal heart rhythm.'

'The school told me he'd just fainted. That there was nothing to worry about but they'd called an ambulance to be on the safe side.'

'It's good that they did. He was in the best place possible when his heart stopped.'

Jason's mother was pale enough to look as though she might be about to faint herself. 'It *stopped*? How? *Why?* Is he going to be okay?'

'That's what we need to find out. Has he ever fainted before? Or had seizures?'

'No…never.'

'Has he been unwell recently? With a virus, perhaps?'

Again, the woman shook her head. She had her gaze fixed on her son's still face now, her fingers pressed against her lips as if she was trying to stifle a sob.

'Is there any chance he's been exposed to drugs?'

'*No...*' She was shocked but then looked fearful. 'They can cause heart attacks, can't they? Some of those pills the kids experiment with these days.'

'Jason hasn't had a heart attack,' Dom explained. 'He's had what we call a sudden cardiac arrest. A heart attack is caused by a blockage in a coronary artery and damage to heart muscle. A heart attack can cause SCA but it's very, very unlikely in Jason's case. It's far more likely that it's been caused by a congenital defect that hasn't shown up before, or a problem with the electrical signal. The cardiologists will be able to tell you a lot more and they'll do whatever tests are necessary to find out the cause.'

'But…but what if it happens again? He…he could die in his sleep or something…'

Tears were escaping now and Jason's mother was getting more and more upset. This wasn't the time to start telling her about implantable defibrillators that could prevent it happening again. She needed reassurance right now. And support.

'Jason's safe here,' Dom told her. 'We're going to take very good care of him but he won't wake up for a little while yet. Would you like to come into one of our relatives' rooms? Can we call family to come and be with you? What about Jason's dad?'

'No...' A handful of tissues was muffling the woman's words. 'It's just me and Jase...' A nurse had come close and put her arm around the distraught mother's shoulders. 'His father hasn't even seen him since he was a baby and my family...well...there's kind of issues there, you know?'

Dom was nodding but he was hearing something else. An echo of Emilia's words.

You have no idea what family issues really are...

The cardiologist team were arriving, Jason was stable and he could see that the boy's mother was going to get plenty of emotional support from his staff so, after a detailed handover to Cardiology, Dom left the resus area. He had other things he needed to do.

He passed the triage desk first.

'Kat? Do you know where Lucas Beaufort is?'

'I heard he's had to take leave to deal with something personal. A family thing, maybe?'

Dom simply nodded and moved on but he was frowning. Why hadn't Lucas come to him to arrange the leave? Did it have something to do with his father, perhaps, and he hadn't wanted to share that with Dom when he was facing a crisis with his own father so critically ill?

Family issues were obviously the theme of the day and the tension that had dissipated to some extent this morning when he'd been told that Roberto's condition was stable was now ramping up again. He had another family member to worry about as well, didn't he? Where was Giada and was she really okay?

In the privacy of his office, Dom hit a speed dial number.

'What's happening?' were her first words. 'Is it Papa?'

'No. The last information I have is that he's stable. Still unconscious but his leg's looking good, his intracranial pressure is under control and everything else is within normal limits. We'll have to be patient. It's a "wait and see" situation.'

'That's what I was told as well. That's why I'm going home.'

'What?' Dom was shocked. 'Home? To Isola Verde? When?'

'I'm on my way now.'

Someone else who was making big decisions and taking leave without even consulting him was disturbing. Surely Giada felt the need to be close to their father at a time like this? She was certainly much closer to him than he was. Or she wanted to be, anyway. And, okay, maybe his little sister had been rebellious enough to cause Roberto some embarrassment years ago but the people of Isola Verde adored her and she'd been the King's right-hand woman for a long time now. It was entirely to Giada's credit that the fabulous new hospital was up and running.

'Someone has to be there,' Giada said into the silence. 'What if this news gets out somehow? Can you imagine the instability it could cause? What if...?' Dom could hear his sister trying to steady her voice. 'What if he dies, Dom?'

'He's stable... He's not in any immediate danger.'

Giada didn't seem to hear him. 'It's *you* who should be going home. You're the person that people need to see. They need to know that you care about the country you're going to rule.'

'I can't just leave.' The feeling of being

torn between two places had been there for so long now, it was very familiar but it was stronger than ever today. Strong enough to be painful. 'And someone needs to be here for Father. He came here for care in my hospital. I'm the one who can ensure that care is the best available.'

'No, Dom…what he really came here for was to talk to you about the succession. To have enough time before his operation to persuade you to come home. In case…in case he didn't survive the surgery.'

'Why didn't you tell me? *Warn* me?' Perhaps Emilia wasn't wrong to find secrets disturbing.

'Papa forbade it. He's afraid, Dom. Of what might happen if people find out before you're back home to take the throne.'

His father…*afraid*…? The concept was alien. He'd always been a somewhat distant figure when the royal children were young and became even more so after their mother had died. Dom hadn't even visited his homeland for years and had barely spoken to his father during that period. Did being afraid meant that Roberto cared about more than his country? That he might have difficulty showing it but he cared about his children? Yesterday's guilt came back with a vengeance.

'I've got to go,' Giada said. 'They're calling our flight.'

'*Our?*'

'It's not a private plane, Dom. Keep in touch, won't you? Let me know if anything changes with Papa. I'll come back as soon as I'm sure everything's fine at home but I can get straight on a flight if I'm needed and be back in twelve hours.'

He had no right to try and persuade her to stay. He had taken himself out of her life as much as their father's when he'd come to America to study and then work.

'Of course I will,' was all he said. 'Safe travels, Gigi.' Using her pet name gave him a lump in his throat. 'I'll miss you.'

He was missing her the moment he ended the call, in fact. He had his father upstairs in the ICU in a coma and the only other family he had was on her way back to Europe. His best friend wasn't available to talk to either. Or was he?

Dom hit another speed dial number but he got a voice mail message that Lucas's phone

was either turned off or reception was un-
available. He left a message.

'Don't know what's up, bro, but I'm here if
you need a friend. Take care.'

Dom dropped his phone on his desk and
rubbed his forehead with his middle finger.
No family to talk to. No best friend. He hadn't
felt this alone for a long, long time. Closing
his eyes, he heard that whisper at the back of
his mind again.

You have no idea...

His eyes snapped open. He had Emilia's
number but he wasn't going to ring, in case
she was busy with a patient. He texted instead.

We got interrupted before. I'd still like to talk.

Discovery Park.

The largest green space in the city and
one of the many great assets that Seattle was
blessed with. There were hundreds of acres of
land with views of the Olympic and Cascade
mountains that were almost as spectacular
as the ones Emilia had seen from the roof of
Seattle General a couple of days ago. There
were miles of beach, dramatic sea cliffs and

sand dunes, forests and streams and, when Emilia didn't have a whole day free that meant she could go as far as the Olympic National Park, or she simply wanted to be available within a reasonable amount of time for any seriously unwell patients, this was the place she always came. She could run, walk or simply sit somewhere to soak in the landscapes she loved and recharge her batteries.

It was normally a solitary activity but Dom's text message yesterday struck her as being almost a plea. Maybe it had been the sincerity of what he'd said about them being so alike, even if that notion was ludicrous given what she'd just learned of his background. Or—and this had been something that had really touched Emilia—it was because he'd said he didn't want to lose what they had. Because it was *real*…

So, she'd texted back and said she had a late start today and, if he had some free time, he was welcome to join her at the park for a jog. And here they were, jogging along a forest track, their breath creating white clouds in the frosty morning air. Emilia was leading the way. Because she knew the tracks of this park so well and where she wanted to go? Or was Dom allowing her to stay in front despite how easy it would be for him to use those long legs of his and turn this into a race? Oddly, that kind of rivalry that could turn anything into a competition was absent this morning. By the time they left the forest track and headed into open space towards the beach and the West Point lighthouse, they were jogging side by side. And then, by tacit consent, they slowed to a walk. In silence to start with, as they both needed to catch their breath.

It was Dom who broke the companionable silence as he turned to smile at Emilia.

'Thanks.'

'What for?'

'Suggesting I come here. I never take advantage of spaces like this when I've only got an hour or two free but this...' He made a sweeping gesture with his arm. 'This is exactly what I needed.'

'It's gorgeous, isn't it? That over there...' Emilia pointed to the snow-capped mountain range in the distance. 'That's the Olympic National Park. If you want to clear your head and put your world to rights properly, then that's the place to go. It takes nearly three hours to get there, though, so I don't go that often but I love it. It's my absolute favourite place in the world, now.'

'I remember you used to love running. You were a real gym bunny back at med school.'

'Only because I couldn't take the time to find places like this.'

'You looked like you were in love with treadmills whenever I got to the gym. I never used the one next to you because you looked like you could keep going for ever and do it faster and steeper than I could,'

Emilia laughed. 'That's what I wanted you to think. The truth was that I was dying inside and was scared that I'd fall flat on my face. Or have a heart attack or something.'

Dom's grin lit up his face. 'Really? It was for my benefit?'

'I was using the old "fake it till you make it" strategy. It was obvious from the get-go that if I wanted to get noticed, you were the one I had to beat.'

'We both pushed each other, that's for sure. I wouldn't have done nearly as well at school if you hadn't been—how do you say it? Setting the post? No…it's setting the bar, I think.'

The tiny slip in his command of American English was unusual enough to remind Emilia that he came from somewhere a long way away. And that that was only one of the differences between them.

'And I might not have even got through school,' she admitted, 'if I hadn't been trying to make sure I got higher marks than you every time.'

'No…' Dom shook his head. 'Everybody knew you were a genius. You were years younger than any of us. You must have done your bachelor's degree while you were still a teenager.'

Emilia shrugged. 'I got fast-tracked. I had a teacher who coached me. Mrs Delaney. She probably saved my life, actually. If it hadn't been for her, I was probably on my way to being in jail. Or dead.' She swallowed hard. 'Like my mom.'

She could hear their feet crunching on stones as they left the path to walk along the beach. Way ahead of them were the cluster of little buildings with the peak of the lighthouse on one of them. Pretty white structures with pink roofs that had the glorious background of the Olympic mountain range behind them.

'Did you have any other family?' Dom asked quietly.

Emilia shrugged. 'Guess I have a father somewhere but I never knew who he was.'

'And your mom really went to jail?'

'Yeah...not until after they took me away when I was five. One of my foster families told me about it later. After they heard she'd died of an overdose as soon as she got out. And then they said that I was going to end up just like her and I'd better behave myself with my next family.'

'Buon delore,' Dom muttered. 'You were just a little girl.' He looked appalled but then, as he held Emilia's gaze, his expression changed to something more like admiration. 'But you won,' he said softly. 'You had such a tough start and yet, here you are—a beautiful woman. An amazing doctor. With the kind of position that you always dreamed of?'

Emilia nodded. 'I have the perfect job. The perfect apartment. And places like this to come to when I'm not at work. I'm very lucky.'

It was true. She *was* very lucky, in every aspect of her life except the most personal but she wasn't about to confess that failure to

Dom. He'd never been short of women who'd been desperate to be his partner, even if it was only a short-lived fling.

'I, too, have been very lucky,' Dom said. 'It always felt too good to be true that I was allowed to come here and study and then to work as a doctor. To be able to do it without anyone knowing who I was made it perfect and it went on for so much longer than I had dreamed it could. I've felt safe. Safe enough to suggest that this was where my father should come for his surgery but now...' He shook his head. 'Now it's falling apart. I may have to leave Seattle General by Christmas. It's past time I stepped up and became King.'

Emilia almost laughed. If someone had told her when she was young that, one day, she would be walking on a beach with a man about to become a king, she would probably have kicked them for teasing her. Here she was, doing it, and it still felt like a fantasy. Too good to be true...?

'I should have done it a long time ago,' Dom added. 'My father is seventy-five. He should have been able to abdicate long ago. He should have had the support of his family to do that. I've been selfish.'

They were almost at the lighthouse now and they both slowed their steps further and then stopped. Emilia could see the guilt that Dom was grappling with. Shame, even, that he'd followed his dream instead of doing his duty?

'You're the one who's an amazing doctor,' she told him. 'Have you ever stopped to count how many people are still alive because of what you gave up and how hard you've worked to become who you really wanted to be? That's not selfish, Dom. It's pretty heroic, if you ask me.'

His expression was changing again and Emilia found herself watching with fascination as she saw frown lines melting and eyes becoming dark with emotion. His smile was barely there, as if he didn't want to take the compliment, but it was so warm it was thanking her for offering comfort.

It still felt too good to be true to be here with this man who was a prince and it also felt incredibly personal. This had to be the first time ever that they'd had a conversation that wasn't about anything professional at all. This wasn't even about the rivalry they'd always fostered.

This was about the connection between them that perhaps neither of them had ever tried to define. The connection that Dom had described as 'real'. It *was* real. And it went deep. It had been brought sharply into focus by the extraordinary revelations of the last couple of days but even more so by Dom saying that he might have to leave Seattle by Christmas. A matter of only weeks away and he was going to vanish from her life for ever and that thought was enough to squeeze Emilia's chest so hard it was impossible to drag in a new breath. As impossible as it was to break that eye contact with Dom.

What this was *really* about was admitting how much she cared for this man, wasn't it? She'd had her suspicions the other day when she'd seen how rattled he was in the ER and again, in his office when she'd appealed for him to tell her the truth about what was going on but this was even bigger.

So big that she knew it was about to shake the foundations of her life.

How ironic was this? To find out that she felt so strongly about Domenico di Rossi when she'd just learned how impossible it was that they could ever be together in any way?

Except…maybe that was precisely why these feelings were bubbling to the surface. Because it was safe.

Because nothing was ever going to happen between them. Or nothing more than what had already happened, anyway. Finally, Emilia was able to drag her gaze away from Dom's. She shifted it to her watch.

'I'm running out of time,' she told him. 'I'll have to run back to the car park. Feel free to take your time, Dom.'

'Ha… I don't think so.'

The way Dom seemed to become even taller reminded her of days long gone when the marks to a quiz or test had been released and her name had been first on the list. He was stepping up to a new challenge. He caught her gaze as they both turned, poised to break into a run and she could see a glimpse of sheer pleasure in his eyes. More than that, even. A new connection because there was more truth between them now?

Whatever. Emilia had a very good reason to stay in front of Dom right now. She didn't want him to guess what had been going through her mind seconds ago. She didn't want to remember it herself and running as fast as possible was a great way to put it behind her. She took off, throwing no more than a smile and a few words over her shoulder.

'Eat my dust…'

CHAPTER FOUR

AN INTENSIVE CARE unit was not the most peaceful place to be for either the patients or the close family members who were beside their beds. The level of staffing was high enough for it to feel crowded and seriously unwell people were there for the constant monitoring they needed which meant they were rarely left alone. The banks of sophisticated monitoring equipment created a background of beeping sounds, occasionally interrupted by alarms as parameters for whatever was being watched reached levels that were too high or low.

Nobody questioned the interest that the head of Seattle General's ER had in this particular patient because he often followed the progress of cases he'd been involved with. Apart from the select few that knew his father's identity, nobody thought there was anything different about the man in the far corner bed who was still in a coma following his emergency surgery for both leg and head injuries. It was a sad thought for Dom that nobody would recognise Roberto Baresi right now, with his head bandaged, eyes puffy and closed and his face half covered with the device securing his breathing tube in place and supporting the bulky connections to the bedside ventilator.

After three days, it was becoming a familiar part of Dom's routine to regularly drop into the ICU. He was also in frequent contact with his father's neurosurgeon, Max Granger, so he could pass on the progress reports to his sister, Giada. During the day, Dom's brief visits were purely clinical, but during the night in Seattle General's post-surgical ICU the staffing level was lower so that was when Dom could spend a little more time by his father's bedside—as a loving son who was grappling with both sadness and guilt at what Roberto was having to endure.

If anybody asked, Dom was going to tell them that he was a friend of the family and the only person close enough to visit, but nobody had asked yet. This was a place where people were ultimately vulnerable so privacy was respected whenever possible to afford patients just a little more dignity.

Dom was sitting quietly now, close to Roberto's bed, in the dimmed lighting of the unit, watching the screens and readouts on the monitors around his father. He was able to speak quietly to him without being overheard thanks to the background hum of the ventilator and the other sounds of the ICU. He told him that Giada was fine and that she was back in Isola Verde and there were no problems at home. He reassured him about the others involved in the accident, telling him that Logan was unhurt and ready to start work next week at Seattle General and that Giorgio was uninjured. He also told him frequently that he was doing well himself. That they were all taking the best care of him and that he was going to come through this with flying colours.

There was still a level of tension, of course. His father had not only survived a serious car accident but had also been through not just one but two life-saving surgeries in the space of only a few hours after that. He was still in a coma and requiring support for his breathing days later with no indications yet of when he might wake up, but there was relief to be found as well. The critical period of the initial six to twelve hours, when a deterioration in clinical status was usually the first sign of a potentially fatal complication, was thankfully well past now and Roberto was stable, with good control of the key aspects of blood pressure and oxygen levels that were so important in the care of a patient with a head injury.

Relief was one of the best feelings in the world, Dom decided, as he let a long, slow breath out, having scanned all the monitors before allowing his gaze to rest on his father's face again. He could actually feel some tension being swept away, to be replaced with a sense of peace that might not last but it was something to be savoured for as long as possible. Dom found himself smiling at his father and leaning closer so he could talk quietly. Not about anything in particular, it was in the hope that his father would be able to hear his voice and to know that someone who loved him was nearby.

'I had a big day in the ER today,' he told Roberto. 'There was just so much going on and a lot of very sick people so I had to try and be in too many places at the same time. There was a shooting victim and someone who'd fallen from a roof. Other people with drug overdoses and heart attacks and someone who was badly burned.' He leaned back to stretch. 'Do you ever get an ache between your shoulder blades from too much stress? Yes...' Dom paused for a long moment, watching his father's face. 'Of course you do. Ruling a country carries a lot more responsibility than running an ER, doesn't it? I have to admit I'm really not looking forward to that at all. The ER is the only kingdom I've ever wanted to rule.'

He let his breath out in a sigh. It was time to change the subject. This might be a one-sided conversation that nobody else could hear but he was still treading on thin ice. If this story broke, the level of tension around Roberto would escalate as private security as well as other measures would have to be installed and that would not help his recovery at all.

'Were the horses your way of defusing the stress? A fast gallop along a beach? The best thing I find is to stand in a really hot shower for a long time. Not that I'd change my job because of the stress, mind you.' He was talking aloud to himself now. He would never have dreamed of saying anything like this to his father if it was a normal conversation. 'I love it because it pushes me to perform the best I can and…when you know you've made a difference—saved a life, possibly—then that's the best feeling in the world. Like relief but bigger…because there's satisfaction in making it happen. Pride, even…'

There was no flicker on his father's face to suggest that he could hear what Dom was saying but it felt good to be telling him how important his job was to him. To say things he should probably have said long ago.

'I've never thanked you for letting me have the opportunity to do this. You could have stopped me from coming here to study in the first place and…and I know you've let me continue working for longer than you wanted to. I'm sorry I haven't been home in so long but it was because I didn't want to have that discussion. I didn't want to feel any more guilty than I already did, that I was putting off doing my duty. Hoping for just another year of being here and being able to be true to myself—as a man. And a doctor. Not as a crown prince who should have stood up to do his duty a long time ago. I've felt so guilty about that…'

Dom let his breath out in another sigh. He shouldn't be talking about this again but it had been bottled up for too long. 'I've felt guilty about keeping the secret of who I am, too. At first it was so good to be able to live like a normal person here and never have to worry about someone taking a picture that might reflect badly on the family but, you know what? Keeping a secret like that meant that nobody really knew me. I think it's actually been a much bigger barrier than I realised. To all sorts of things…'

Because there was the most astonishing relief to be found in the fact that Emilia Featherstone now knew that secret. He'd always been himself with her—or what he thought of as his real self—but that secret was also part of himself and it had created a solid wall between them. A gap that could never be bridged. Now it was gone and, while the smashing of that barrier had created a bit of damage and he couldn't blame Emilia for having been so angry he was hopeful that, given time, she would trust him again and they would be on new ground.

Astonishing new ground, for both of them, but most significantly, for Dom.

He'd never had a relationship with anyone that felt as honest as the one he had with Emilia. She'd never held back, either in competing with him all through medical school or giving as good as she got in their personal banter that was often a little too close to being insulting to be acceptable with any other people and totally unthinkable with anyone he might interact with as a prince.

A nurse came into the space Dom was occupying by his father's bedside. 'Excuse me, Dr Di Rossi, but I need to take an arterial blood sample to check Mr Baresi's oxygen levels. We're due to reposition him soon, as well.'

'Of course. I'll get out of your way.'

'There's no need—it won't take too long and it's nice to see Mr Baresi with some company. It's sad that his family can't be with him.'

'Mmm...' Dom stood up as he made the noncommittal sound. 'It is. But I can't stay any longer. It's good to see that he's stable.

He's doing well, given all that he's dealing with.'

The nurse smiled, nodding, as she moved in with the small syringe to take a sample of blood from the arterial line—one of the many ways his father's condition was being monitored closely. Dom left the unit. It was late but he was going to go back to his office in the ER and catch up on some paperwork, his head a lot clearer now that some of the day's tension had evaporated.

Taking the stairs instead of an elevator, Dom found his thoughts tracking back to Emilia again. To the unique relationship they had that wasn't exactly friendship but it was, nevertheless, remarkably close. His friendship with Lucas was the closest relationship he'd ever had with anyone outside his family and that had been forged from the things they had in common. They were both men who had issues with what was expected of them by their families. They worked together. They relaxed together whenever they could, over a beer and a pizza. They were like brothers— they had each other's backs and, while they might have disagreements, ultimately they were on the same side.

His and Emilia's history was pretty much the opposite. Years of battling with each other to be seen as the best. An unspoken understanding that it was of the utmost importance to succeed and it hadn't mattered that neither of them had known exactly why it was so important to the other.

For Dom, it had been about being true to himself.

And for Emilia? Had it been about escaping her background?

He pushed open the internal doors to the ER and walked through a department that was quiet enough for the moment to seem a totally different world from the space he'd been working in all day. There were no distractions on the way to his office that disrupted his train of thought.

He and Emilia were actually far more alike than he'd realised. They'd both been escaping their backgrounds. Okay, from the outside, it would look like they were total opposites because she was escaping poverty and the lack of anyone who cared about who she was or what her future might hold and he'd been surrounded by unlimited wealth and people who cared too much about who he was and a future that was inescapable.

But…at a level that was soul-deep, they were kind of the same thing, weren't they?

And if Emilia could see that, maybe she would forgive him for having kept that secret. Not that it should matter so much but… it did…

Because he'd never had a relationship with anyone that was like what he had with Emilia and he certainly would never get the chance to have another one when he stepped up to take on his responsibilities as King. Knowing that he was soon going to lose what he was only just discovering was disturbing because it felt…important. Special.

The paperwork on his desk was ignored. Dom pulled out his phone instead. It was after midnight and it would be rude to wake someone up by sending a text message… But that feeling of something important about his relationship with Emilia was morphing into a sense of almost urgency.

Have just realised it's almost Thanksgiving. Do you have plans for dinner?

Her response came swiftly enough to let him know she hadn't been asleep.

Ha-ha. I've always thought I should cook a turkey and a pumpkin pie, etc., etc., but I've never been inspired.

Can you actually cook?

A lot better than you, I expect.

Want to put that to the test?

There was a minute's silence but then Dom's lips curved into a smile as her response pinged in because it felt like normal service was being resumed, here, between himself and Emilia. A bit of banter. A whole lot of friendly competition.

I'll do the turkey. You do the pumpkin pie. Your place or mine?

Mine. And bring the ingredients so we know there's no cheating and buying ready-made.

Don't need to cheat, mate. I'll be surprised if you can even boil water.

An emoji of a winking face had been added to the end of her message.

Wanting something that you knew you were never likely to have was like pressing your nose against a glass window as you gazed longingly at what you could see on the other side.

For Emilia Featherstone, the sense of desperately wanting what other people all seemed to have but was always out of reach for herself was almost a comforting feeling because it was so familiar. Because she knew that she'd experienced it often enough in her lifetime to know that, no matter how overwhelming it might seem, she could deal with it. She would probably end up being stronger because of it, in fact.

The most overwhelming longings were the emotional things, of course.

The need to belong somewhere. The need to be loved. The kind of windows that were always lit up extra brightly around celebrations for Thanksgiving or Christmas—those family celebrations when everybody else seemed to be enfolded in loving gatherings.

Maybe there was a new longing Emilia

could add this year—the need to be with the person that *she* loved?

No…she needed to qualify that. It wasn't just a random need to be with someone she cared deeply about, it was a specific need to be with Domenico di Rossi. It wasn't just an aftershock of realising how much she cared about him because this was very different from having a crush on someone, or even falling in love. She'd been in love before and, although her last relationship had carried on for far longer than it should have and any memories were now tainted, Emilia knew that even at the beginning it had been nothing like this.

She'd never felt connected to anyone in quite the way she did now to Dom. But the glass in this new window was impossibly thick. It wasn't simply the idea of a relationship that was equal enough to have respect on both sides, or to be able to trust the other with a raw honesty that made the connection tight enough to be unbreakable, it was the whole royalty thing. As crazy as it seemed, Dom was a *prince*. Soon to become a *king*. And that was enough to make that window so thick it actually felt like a safety barrier. Or one of those glass bridges they had in places like China where you could walk over a chasm and experience the thrill but know that you were perfectly safe and that you could trust that the glass was never going to break.

So maybe that was why Emilia was here now. In Dom's apartment. Taking over the bench space while he'd marked out his own territory on the huge island countertop. A double oven was already heating up. So was their impending battle over who was the better cook. Emilia eyed up the raw turkey in front of her. She'd sat up last night, watching videos online that promised to teach her how to cook the perfect roast turkey for Thanksgiving dinner and she had all the supplies she needed. She pulled on kitchen gloves before tackling a task she'd never been partial to as she unwrapped and then used paper towels to dry the poultry.

'If I had to do this on a regular basis, I'd probably become a vegetarian,' she muttered, tying the legs of the large bird together with a piece of string.

'Want to swap? You can make the pies.'

'Pie*s*?' Emilia emphasised the last letter of the word. 'Plural?'

'*Sì.*' Dom was tying the strings of his

apron. 'My research told me that it was compulsory to have both an apple and a pumpkin pie on the table for dessert. I think my task is going to be harder than yours.'

'Doubt it.' Emilia pushed the turkey's ugly neck and tail skin out of sight and tucked the wings beneath the body to provide the platform for roasting that one of the videos had recommended. 'It's not just the turkey, you know. There are all the side dishes to do and gravy to make.' She dribbled olive oil over the turkey and rubbed it over the skin with her hands. 'Garlic mashed potatoes, cranberry sauce, Brussels sprouts, green beans—'

'Enough…' Dom was grinning. 'I declare the competition on even ground and I don't want to swap any more. Here, let me pour you a glass of wine.' He reached for the bottle of red wine amongst the grocery bags still on the floor. 'Were you really telling the truth when you said you'd never cooked a turkey before? At least I have the excuse of not being American.'

'I don't tell lies.' The words came out sounding curt and Emilia bit her lip as she saw the wary look that crossed Dom's face. 'Sorry…' She stripped off her gloves before taking the glass of wine he was holding out towards her. 'I'm not accusing you of lying.'

'But I kept my secret and that's just as bad, yes?' Dom held her gaze. 'No more secrets, Emmy, I promise. Not ever...'

The thought that 'not ever' might not be very long at all was enough to make Emilia's breath catch in her throat. At some point in the near future, Dom was going to disappear from her life and why on earth would the ruler of a small Mediterranean kingdom have any desire to keep in touch with someone from a life he'd had to leave far behind? But there was something in that sombre gaze that told Emilia that the connection would always be there. They shared a passion for what they did in life. They also shared a passion for competing with each other and there was something close enough to sadness in Dom's eyes to let her know that he was going to miss so much of his life here. The high-paced drama that the ER could provide. Perhaps he was realising that he would miss the connection they had, as well.

Would miss *her*...?

Emilia took a sip of her wine to force herself to break that eye contact. To try and distract herself from the swirl of emotion that was threatening to distract her completely. It worked. She found herself blinking in surprise, in fact.

'Oh, wow…that's the nicest wine I've ever tasted.'

'We have some of the best vineyards in Europe on Isola Verde.' Dom smiled. 'And we make the best olive oil and you should taste the limoncello.' He raised his own glass to touch Emilia's. 'Maybe you will someday.'

'Mmm…' Emilia drowned her response with another mouthful of wine but then she put her glass down to reach for the herbs and other seasoning that she was going to use on the turkey. 'I'll have this in the oven in a minute,' she announced. 'The countdown is on. You've only got a few hours to get those pies made and baked. I hope you didn't cheat and buy ready-made pastry?'

The sound Dom made was indignant. 'As if…'

A short time later, the black granite top of the central island bench was a snowstorm of flour to one side where there were several bowls being devoted to pastry making and there was a pumpkin being carved into pieces on the other side. Impressively, Dom was clearly intending to make his pumpkin purée from scratch. When he'd got all the pieces into a pot to boil, he refilled their wine glasses.

'This is nice,' he declared. 'It's good to be away from the hospital for a while.'

Emilia nodded. 'I imagine you're spending a lot of extra time there at the moment.'

'I read an interesting article about talking to people when they are in a coma. There was a study, from back in 2015, I think, where brain scans revealed that some coma patients can hear and understand what is spoken around them. The people who had family members speaking to them every day woke up significantly faster and had a better recovery. So, yes… I visit him as often as I can.'

'How's he doing?'

It was safe ground to discuss Roberto's condition in medical terms and both Dom and Emilia could carry on with their tasks as they talked about every detail of the care Dom's father was receiving. Emilia made cranberry sauce as they debated the pros and cons of an early tracheostomy for patients who were going to need prolonged control of their ventilation.

'It's only been five days. Early is anything up to ten days so we can afford to wait longer.'

'Doesn't an early tracheostomy have benefits in shortening the duration of mechanical ventilation and minimising risks of weaning failure?'

'Yes, but why do such an invasive procedure if it's not absolutely necessary? They're already starting the gradual reduction of ventilatory support. I'm hoping that my father's spontaneous breathing will be adequate before long. He's tough.' Dom looked as though he was focussing hard on rolling out his pastry. 'Determined. He's going to succeed in this fight.' He was blinking rapidly now and his voice was trailing into silence. 'He's going to win...'

'Like father, like son.'

'*Scusi?*' Dom looked puzzled.

'You're very alike, I think. You and your father. You both like to win.'

His lips curved into a hint of a smile. 'You could be right. And, this time, I *am* going to win. You're going to be blown away by what

I'm about to do.' He was picking up a sharp knife. And…a ruler?

'Well, I'm about to make the best gravy in the world.' Emilia found her phone and did a quick search for a recipe she had bookmarked. Moments later, however, she was searching through her grocery bags.

'What are you looking for?' Dom looked up from where he was slicing his pastry into thin strips.

'I need to make stock. The recipe says to boil the neck of my turkey as a base but my turkey didn't *have* a neck.'

'It will be in a plastic bag. With all the other giblets.'

Giblets? Emilia wasn't going to admit she had no idea what that meant. 'I have everything else I need, like flour and sage. I might have to go back to the butcher and ask what happened to the neck.'

'I wouldn't bother. Have a look in the pantry. There's bound to be some ready-made stock in there. My housekeeper often cooks for me and leaves meals for when I need them so there are all sorts of things on the shelves. Chicken stock would do fine, I expect.'

Emilia scowled. 'Ready-made is cheating.'

Dom's smile widened. 'I'll let you off. It's not as if you're going to win, anyway. Look at this work of art.' He had his pastry strips laid across a pie plate filled with sliced apples and he was somehow weaving them into a very professional looking lattice. 'Oops…that goes over, not under. Stop distracting me, Emmy. I need to get these into the oven so we don't have to wait for dessert later.'

Funny how Emilia had always hated anyone calling her 'Emmy'. She was actually liking it today. Liking it a lot. As much as she was enjoying the cooking. And then setting the table later as the aromas from the roasting meat and vegetables and the bubbling gravy and sauce became delicious enough to make her feel very hungry. It smelt like Thanksgiving and, for the first time ever, it felt like she was a real part of it.

It felt like she belonged.

This sleek, modern apartment that had been chosen for its proximity to Seattle General provided a level of luxury that made life outside work comfortable enough for Dom that he was never distracted from his focus on his career.

Mind you, it had never looked like this, with dishes and pots piling up in the sink and surfaces covered with the remnants of the impromptu cooking competition. It had never smelt quite like this, either, with the savoury aromas of roasting meat and bubbling gravy having their own competition with the sweeter scent of baked goods coming from the oven he was using. Dom crouched down to peer through the glass door of the oven. He was going to turn it off very soon to make sure the pastry didn't get too brown on top and that the pies had time to cool before they ate them. Emilia had finished setting the table and she was about to mash potatoes. Another appetising aroma got added to the mix as she squeezed roasted garlic cloves into the pot. Dom found the fresh cream in his fridge that he needed to whip to go with his pies. Nothing was coming out of a can, today.

'I'm starving,' he told Emilia a little later, putting the whipped cream back in the fridge.

'Me, too. This has all taken a lot longer than I thought it would.'

'And I've been boring you talking shop. I think you're as clued up on my father's condition as anybody in his medical team.'

'I'm not bored, Dom. Of course he's on your mind. He's your father and I can understand how worried you must be. It's easy to see how much you love him.'

Was it?

Dom watched as Emilia took the foil covering off the turkey that had been resting on the bench. He'd been driven by his concern for his father ever since Roberto had been wheeled into his ER and his fear had been mixed with a huge amount of guilt for having ducked his own responsibilities for so long. He was trying to keep in touch with his sister and reassure her and trying to ensure that their father knew that they cared but... Emilia had hit the nail on the head with that one, tiny word, hadn't she?

He *did* love his father. And maybe that love had got buried under resentment that the career he loved was eventually going to be taken away from him and the distance that had been created had added another layer that muffled that love, but the near catastrophe of the accident had shattered those barriers.

'You're very lucky, you know.' Emilia's smile was soft as she looked up to catch his gaze. 'You've got a family to be thankful for and that's what Thanksgiving is all about. Family is everything, isn't it?'

She broke their shared gaze and seemed to be blinking hard. 'Now...look at this.' She moved a magnificently browned turkey onto a wooden board. 'You may as well concede defeat, Dom. Have you ever seen anything that looks this good?'

'It does look good.' His tone was cautious, however. Dom wasn't about to let Emilia think she'd won already. And he was still thinking about those softly spoken words that sounded as if they'd come straight from the heart.

Family is everything, isn't it?

He was lucky. He had a father and a sister and a wonderful home waiting for him on a sun-drenched Mediterranean island. How close had Emilia ever been to feeling like she had a family? Or a real home, for that matter? If he'd known more about her years ago, would that have changed their relationship?

He watched as Emilia gathered the other dishes to take to the table. Tendrils of her hair had come loose to float around her face and the glow on her cheeks almost matched the fiery tones of her hair. She had her sleeves

rolled up and her apron was grubby and…
and she'd never looked as lovely as she did
right now.

It took Dom back to the first time he'd ever
seen her. When he'd recognised that she presented a risk to his focus. What a relief it
had been to find that she was so determined
to outdo him and that nothing personal was
going to be allowed to interfere with that
goal. So, no. It wouldn't have changed their
relationship because that wouldn't have been
allowed. And now it *had* changed, because
there was truth between them but it was too
late because this was the beginning of the end
of his life here in Seattle. Very soon it would
be time for him to re-join the family he was
lucky enough to have but, in the meantime,
he could enjoy this celebration.

They ate in silence for several minutes.

'Potatoes are good,' he told Emilia. 'And
the beans. I even like the sprouts.'

'But…?'

'Um… I hate to say it…'

'But you're going to, anyway.' Emilia
sighed heavily as she put her fork down. 'And
you're right. The turkey tastes weird.'

'It does a bit.'

'What's wrong with it?'

'I don't know.' Dom ate another mouthful, staring at the rest of the turkey on its board. 'It almost tastes like…plastic.' He could feel himself frowning as his gaze sharpened. 'What's that?'

'What?'

He reached to take hold of what he'd spotted on the carving board. 'You didn't put stuffing in this turkey, did you?'

Emilia shook her head. 'I read that it can be a risk for food poisoning.'

'So what's this?'

Her mouth dropped as he pulled it out.

'What *is* that?'

Dom was laughing now. 'You know how you couldn't find the bag of giblets when you were looking for the neck? Did you think of looking inside the turkey?'

'No…that's gross. Why would you put a plastic bag in there? Hey…*stop*…' Emilia leaned far enough to thump his arm. 'Stop laughing at me.'

But she was having trouble not smiling herself and Dom couldn't stop. Even when he caught the smoke seeping out of the oven from the corner of his eye, moments before the alarm sounded, he was still laughing. He'd forgotten to turn the oven off, hadn't he? His pies weren't going to be too brown, they were probably incinerated by now.

In the space of what felt like seconds, their Thanksgiving dinner had become an epic disaster.

So why on earth did he feel like he was having what could possibly be the best time of his life?

CHAPTER FIVE

IT WAS STARTING.

As always, the end of Thanksgiving celebrations was the signal for the Christmas season to begin. Conversations in the staffroom included queries about who would be entering the annual Christmas cookie competition that was approaching and reminders that the last tickets for the fundraiser gala ball on the twelfth of December were being snapped up so people needed to hurry if they wanted to attend the glamorous event. Snatches of Christmas music could be heard already in the cafés and shops, and decorations began appearing in corners of departments and wards throughout Seattle General.

It only became official on the first day of December, however, with the installation of Christmas trees in the hospital's huge, glass-walled atrium. One massive spruce tree stretched high into the impressive space of this entrance, with a slightly smaller tree beside it, both wearing identical decorations of sparkling, white fairy lights, frosted glass icicles and silver balls of various sizes. Beneath the trees there was thick, fluffy, white fabric bunched up to look like drifts of snow.

Not that Emilia was taking any notice of the trees as she rushed past, cheeks still glowing from the early run she and Dom had completed at the park. Her trauma team pager had sounded as she pulled on a clean set of scrubs in the orthopaedic department's surgical locker room but, even if she wasn't already totally focussed on what might be waiting for her in the ER, she would have ignored the blatant symbols of the upcoming celebration. Memories of Thanksgiving days in her childhood were insignificant compared to those surrounding Christmas Day and none of them were happy memories. Emilia had learned that the joy of Christmas was for other people. For children who had their own families. Who were wanted. And loved...

The decorations and the music of the season, festive flashing jewellery and headbands with reindeer antlers or Santa hats attached, gift wrapping and special food were all part of a background clutter that she could ignore or tolerate for a few weeks of every year. It didn't even bother her particularly now. In the same way that Emilia had learned that standing out from the crowd in terms of academic achievement could change your life for the better, she was well practised in the art of distracting herself from any personal emotional disturbance by using mindfulness. And there couldn't be a better way of being entirely present than being involved in the fight to save someone's life.

Becoming totally involved was inevitable from the moment Emilia arrived in the ER. Due to it being a shift change-over period, with the department already busy, things were more chaotic than usual. On top of that, there seemed to have been little warning that a serious trauma case was on its way. The ambulance had already arrived and the patient was being rushed into Resus as both Emilia and Dom came through the doors. Dom probably wasn't even due to start his shift yet and he looked as if he'd not long stepped out of a shower. It also looked like he'd towel dried his hair but hadn't had a chance to comb it.

The thought that looking unusually tousled achieved what should have been impossible— in that it instantly increased the man's attractiveness—was fleeting enough to be no more than a blink as Emilia reached for a pair of gloves from the wall dispenser at the same moment as Dom. They caught each other's gazes for a heartbeat and it was a relief for Emilia that there was nothing personal in that shared glance, like any awareness of appearance or perhaps the recognition of how much closer they'd become in the days since that shared Thanksgiving dinner disaster or even how much more time they'd been spending together. The silent message that flashed between them was a very different kind of recognition. One that acknowledged a shared determination to do their best for this patient, no matter what they might be up against.

Dom snapped his gloves on as he turned towards the ambulance crew. 'Talk to me,' he commanded, stepping closer to the gurney.

'This is a gentleman in his early seventies, we believe. Name's Brian Butcher.' The paramedic leaned down as his patient groaned loudly. 'It's okay, Brian. We're at the hospital. Try not to move…'

His junior crew partner took over. 'Fall from height,' he told Dom. 'Maybe fifteen feet? He was up on his roof, putting one of those Santa Claus decorations up—the ones where it's just the legs sticking out of the chimney, you know?'

It only took a quirk of Dom's eyebrow to let the EMT know that it was only the clinical details that were needed urgently.

'The fall was partially broken by shrubbery but he landed on a concrete driveway,' the senior paramedic continued. 'GCS was eight on arrival with eye opening to pain, incomprehensible speech and withdrawal to pain. Blood pressure of ninety systolic, tachycardic at one thirty. Initial IV access failed and we were so close we decided it was better to just load and go.'

Emilia had her gloves on now and she also stepped closer. She could understand that IV access had probably been difficult due to the obesity of this patient. It could mean that airway management would also prove challenging but the immediate concern was getting enough staff on hand to move him from the gurney to the bed. Where was everybody?

She and Dom had been joined by an intern and two nurses but there were people missing.

'Lucas back yet?' Dom asked. 'Is he with the team in Resus One dealing with that bus versus pedestrian?'

'No. But I can see if they can spare anyone,' a nurse responded.

'Who's rostered to take his place on airway management for the trauma team?'

'Didn't you pencil in the new guy that's starting today?' The intern asked. 'Logan somebody? I don't think he's arrived yet, though.'

'Connors,' Dom murmured. 'But I wouldn't throw him in the deep end like this. Not on his first day, anyway. I was expecting Lucas would be back to get him up to speed with the team.' He shook his head, as if dismissing information that was no more than a distraction. 'I'll do it. Grab a sliding board and see if anyone else is nearby to help for a minute. Let's get Brian onto the bed, stat. I'm not liking the sound of that stridor.'

The noisy breath sounds were a warning that the man's airway was becoming obstructed which could be due to factors such as swelling, bleeding or aspiration of possibly broken teeth. Whatever the cause, stabilising the airway and breathing were the first steps of any major trauma management and this patient was going to be a real challenge.

One that Dom was clearly up for. He was already observing Brian for any further signs of respiratory difficulty as he directed the limited team he had, including the ambulance crew for the moment, to remove clothing, get monitors in place for heart rate and rhythm, blood pressure and oxygen saturation and to stabilise the cervical spine as the hard collar was opened to let him examine the mouth and neck.

'I need some suction here, please.' He took the handle attached to the device from the nurse as he turned back to the paramedic. 'Do we know anything about his medical history?'

The paramedic shook his head. 'No medic alert bracelet. He lives alone but his neighbour—Dierdre—was going to check his house and bring some stuff in for him. We asked her to check for any medication he might be on.'

Dom nodded, peering into the injured man's mouth after clearing the blood that had been obstructing his vision but he looked up to catch Emilia's gaze as Brian's padded jacket and then a knitted sweater and T-shirt were all cut clear to expose the top half of his body.

'Flail chest,' she noted aloud. The paradoxical movement of the ribs that went in the opposite direction than they should as a breath was sucked in or released meant that there were multiple fractures that had separated a section of the rib cage from the rest. It was also a sign that the level of difficulty in stabilising this patient might have just gone up several notches.

'We've got accessory muscle use and tachypnoea as well.' Dom was frowning as the figures on the monitor appeared. 'And that oxygen saturation is far too low. We need to intubate. I'm going to need the video laryngoscope,' he told the intern. 'And let's have a cricothyroidotomy kit on standby as well, thanks. Emmy, it would be awesome if you could get IV access while I'm getting the drugs drawn up. And then I'd like you to assist me with the intubation, please.'

Emilia knew that Dom probably had no idea he'd used the familiar version of her name but, if anything, it just cemented the bond they needed to work as closely and rapidly as possible right now with their patient's condition deteriorating in front of them. Just the first step of stabilising this patient by securing IV access and an airway was a battle that would require their best efforts.

It wasn't her usual role on this team, of course. Her specialist orthopaedic and trauma skills meant that she should be evaluating that chest and looking for any other life-threatening injuries a fall could have produced, such as a fractured pelvis, but she couldn't move on to that stage of a primary or secondary survey until the patient was able to breathe. It was a matter of priorities. Even trying to keep the alignment of Brian's neck completely stable was less important than securing an airway because the risk of brain injury from a lack of oxygen was greater than making a spinal injury worse by extending the neck for intubation.

The next few minutes were chaotic. Staff were still removing the last pieces of clothing, getting ECG leads stuck on and manoeuvring the trolleys that were needed to supply the drugs and medical equipment that were about to be used. Dom was drawing up the drugs that would sedate and paralyse Brian so that they could take over his breathing. Emilia had the IV trolley beside her and she was trying to locate a vein she could access so that those drugs could be administered. It was no easy task but if they needed to place a central line or an intraosseus needle directly into bone marrow, it would take time they might not have.

There was a fair amount of luck that coated whatever skills Emilia used to find a vein so she could hook Brian up to a running line of saline. The glance and nod of approval from Dom when she looked up was all the acknowledgment she needed to know that she'd done well. Now it was time to do everything she could to assist Dom in his task of placing a flexible, plastic tube into Brian's trachea to ensure that adequate levels of oxygen could be delivered to Brian's lungs.

As the first drugs were administered, Emilia pre-oxygenated using a bag mask, making sure that everything needed was at hand and that the monitor could be easily seen.

The first attempt to insert the tube did fail. 'Let's optimise the position,' Dom said calmly. 'I want a thirty-degree tilt on the upper body so that we have the ears in line with the sternal notch. I'll try a different blade and, Emilia, I'm going to need some anterior tracheal pressure, please.'

Emilia had to locate the cricoid cartilage, stabilise it between her fingers and then apply enough pressure to help Dom slide the tube into the correct position. She had to keep holding that pressure, as well, until the position of the tube had been checked.

She could see the mix of satisfaction and relief on Dom's face as they confirmed that the airway was in place but his focus didn't slip for a second because, with the pressure of air entering their patient's lungs, it became obvious that the rib fractures had caused damage. Either air or blood was in the chest cavity to a degree that would prevent adequate oxygenation and this was as life-threatening as not having a patent airway.

As a surgeon, Emilia took the lead on the next urgent task of inserting a chest tube to clear the obstruction and this time, as a rush of blood confirmed that her incision and blunt dissection had reached the pleural space and that they could deal with the problems the bleeding was causing, there was more than a fleeting gleam of satisfaction when Dom's gaze caught her own as he helped her secure the tube that would continue the drainage.

The figures on the monitors were already improving enough that they both knew the odds were turning in their favour. They still needed to perform a thorough secondary survey and find whatever other injuries Brian might have sustained and he was very likely to need to go to Theatre soon but it felt like they were winning.

As always, this was the best feeling in the world.

Their eye contact held for a heartbeat longer than it might have, even as recently as a week or two ago. Because Dom knew that she knew more than she had before? Because they had acknowledged their connection? She could hear an echo of his voice in that tiny moment of time their gazes were touching.

'We're the same, you and me... We both give everything we've got—and more—to our careers. To the people who put their trust and their lives into our hands...'

How hard was it going to be for Dom to walk away from this job? It would have to feel like he was cutting out a piece of his heart—his soul, even—and a piece of Emilia's heart was breaking for him because she could imagine exactly how hard that would be. She couldn't do it.

But, however alike they were in how much they loved their jobs and how determined they were to be the best, that was where their similarity ended, wasn't it? It was when Brian's neighbour, Dierdre, arrived with a plastic bag of medication she'd found in his bathroom cabinet and his wallet containing all the personal details they would need that Emilia was reminded of how different she and Dom really were.

Unlike their patient—and herself—Dom had a family. And, okay, there were some issues there because Dom was expected to do something that wasn't what he would have chosen to do with his life and it was a very different kind of family from that of an ordinary person but at the end of the day…it was *family* and, as she had reminded Dom on Thanksgiving, family was everything. So, there was envy mixed in with that sympathy that Dom was going to have to give up the career that he loved so much in the near future. On top of that, as Emilia prepared to accompany Brian first to a CT scan and then to Theatre, she remembered that weird moment when she'd arrived in the ER earlier, when the sight of Dom's tousled hair had made her aware of something so inappropriately unprofessional that she was ashamed of herself.

Oh, man…life had been a lot less complicated when the only feelings that Domenico Di Rossi inspired had been those that made her so determined to prove herself and earn his—along with everybody else's—respect. Even the annoyance that his teasing and the forbidden use of that shortened form of her name had created would be preferable to this…this *knot* of emotion that seemed to have taken up residence deep in her gut, full of things she could almost, but not quite identify clearly. And Emilia had no intention of trying to analyse them any further. What was the point, when they would be irrelevant before very long anyway? And when admitting something could potentially make it real…?

It was a relief to be able to follow Brian's trolley through the doors and head for the elevators. She would be in the CT scanning room within minutes and, with the information the scan could provide, would be planning what was going to happen a short time later in Theatre—a place where she could make sure she was in control. A place where unsettling personal emotions could be totally, albeit perhaps only temporarily, banished.

Exactly the place Emilia needed to be as soon as possible. She knew that Dom was watching her leave Resus but she deliberately kept her gaze on the monitor attached to the end of the trolley so that she didn't look back. She didn't want to notice that tousled hair again, or to have that link from those dark, dark eyes to her own, even for a heartbeat. She didn't want to feel any of those emotions that were powerful enough to feel physical.

Weird how hard it was not to turn her head, though...

What a day...

It was well after the time his shift should have ended when Dom managed to get in a visit to his father in ICU and it was only then that he realised he'd missed lunch. After the extra physical activity of that run with Emilia early this morning, it was no wonder that he was experiencing symptoms of hypoglycaemia with a headache and vague dizziness but Dom knew that a coffee with a couple of sugars would keep him going until he could get home.

He paused for a moment on his way to the ICU staffroom, however, because something had been niggling at the back of his mind ever since that dramatic case in the ER this morning. Why wasn't Lucas back from his unexpected leave of absence yet? And what could be serious enough have kept him away for this long already?

He'd had a response to that voicemail he'd left the day Lucas had disappeared, more than a week ago now, but all Lucas had said was that he had some stuff to sort out and that he'd be in touch soon.

Not knowing where on earth his friend was, and what time zone he might be in, Dom sent a text message this time instead of trying to phone. He also tried to make it clear he didn't want to pry.

You missed a good case this morning, bro. Flail chest, haemopneumothorax and a challenging airway thrown in just for fun. You would've loved it.

Surprisingly, a response pinged back by the time Dom had started walking again.

Sounds like you're having fun, all right. I'm sure you're coping without me but I'll be back soon. In time for the ball at the latest, if you can remember to grab me a ticket.

It was reassuring that he'd been able to make contact so easily but Dom still had no idea where Lucas was or what the problem in his life might be. Should he be worried? Or was the fact that Lucas was even thinking of attending a social function enough to reassure him that it couldn't be anything too serious?

He was still distracted as he reached the ICU staffroom and suddenly he had to pause again, startled enough to completely let go of his train of thought concerning Lucas. Emilia Featherstone was in the staffroom, paperwork spread out in front of her on the table.

'What on earth are you doing here?'

'I've got a patient in ICU. Our man from this morning who fell off his roof. Two, actually, if we count your...' Emilia's eyes widened as she stopped herself. 'Your...um... patient Mr Baresi.'

A glance over his shoulder showed Dom that there was nobody around who might overhear their conversation, but it was an automatic instinct to be extra careful at work.

'His leg seems to be healing well.'

'It is. And Max Granger seems happy enough with how stable he is neurologically.'

'Mmm… I'll be a lot happier when he wakes up.' Dom closed his eyes in a long blink. 'It's been a long day. I just came in for a coffee. And maybe a cookie. I forgot lunch.'

'What? You must be dead on your feet. Look, there's a whole box of cookies here. I think someone's practising for the competition.'

'Gingerbread men?' Dom picked up one of the cookies.

'No…turn it up the other way. It's a reindeer.'

Dom peered at the shape. A gingerbread man cutter had clearly been used but it had been decorated so that the legs were antlers, the arms were ears and there was a red candy button for a nose where the head would have been.

'Clever,' he murmured, biting off one of the antlers. 'How's our man from this morning?'

'Good.' Emilia was gathering her paperwork. 'I'm just sorting copies of the data I need to enter him in an ongoing study for surgical stabilisation of rib fractures.'

Dom took another bite. 'I'm going to blame my lack of brain function on low blood sugar. I was just reading about it the other day. About bioabsorbable plates for a fixation device?'

'I used a pre-contoured locking plate,' Emilia told him but there was a gleam in her eye. 'We can compare the merits some other time, when you've had enough to eat.'

'These cookies are good.'

That gleam in Emilia's eyes got brighter. 'Your baking skills are pretty unique. Why don't you enter the competition?'

Dom ate the reindeer's nose. 'Why don't you? There could be someone on the judging panel that appreciates plastic-flavoured Christmas cookies.'

She was having difficulty stifling a grin. 'That's a cruel blow, Dom. You could be doing irreparable damage to my self-esteem, you know?'

Maybe it was the lighting in this staffroom and the way it was picking out the flame-coloured highlights in Emilia's hair and making her eyes sparkle. Or maybe it was because something fundamental had changed in their relationship ever since he had told her the truth and she'd got past her initial shock and anger. On the other hand, it could be that his mental abilities were foggy thanks to a lack of food and those automatic defence mechanisms had been accidentally switched off. Whatever the cause, the net result hit Dom in the gut like a sledgehammer. Emilia had to be the most attractive woman he'd ever met. How on earth had he not noticed that before?

The kick in his gut was rapidly morphing into something Dom had certainly noticed before.

Attraction.

No…worse than that. This was more like *desire*…

The last thing he needed in his life right now was another complication. He should walk away. Fast. Except that Emilia was saying something. About food…? He tuned back in and tried to rewind what he'd missed.

'I haven't tried it yet but it sounds good.' A tiny, puzzled frown appeared on Emilia's brow as she clocked how distracted he was.

'The new Asian fusion restaurant down at the Pike Place Fish Market?' Those astonishing blue eyes were darkening with what looked like concern now. 'Boy, you really do need some food, don't you? Come on…it's time we were out of here. My treat.'

'What? No… I'm not letting you pay for dinner.' Had he somehow just agreed to have dinner with Emilia—only seconds after realising that it would be wise to get away from her until his head was functioning a little more normally?

'Consider it compensation.' Emilia was on her feet smiling at him. 'To make up for plastic-flavoured turkey?'

The gingerbread cookie didn't seem to have raised his blood sugar levels enough to dispel the fuzziness in his head. Or perhaps Emilia's smile always had this kind of effect on men and it was just that his own immunity was compromised. In either case, the net result was that he was powerless to resist.

'Dinner sounds great,' he heard himself saying. 'Let's go.'

He'd looked so tired. And then he'd said that he hadn't eaten all day. Was it any wonder that Emilia had let her concern for Dom override her common sense? That she'd not only smothered any warning bells about letting that emotional knot get pulled any tighter, she'd made it a whole lot more intense by engineering time alone with him in a restaurant that allowed every table a view into a bustling kitchen but somehow divided the spaces to make every group feel like they were having a private party.

They both seemed to be making an effort to keep things at least a little professional, though, with their conversation focussed on the case they'd shared today as they waited for their order to arrive.

'So, tell me about this study that Brian qualifies for. You said it's ongoing? What trends are being identified?'

'Initially, the study was looking at surgical stabilisation compared to the conservative, non-surgical treatment that was standard a couple of decades ago.'

'Like oral analgesia, mechanical ventilation and intercostal nerve blocks?'

Emilia nodded. 'But now, it's more about how early the surgery should take place. The benefits are significant—lower mortality, shorter stay in ICU and less time under mechanical ventilation. Lower rates of pneumonia…'

She was counting off her points on her fingers but Dom wasn't watching her hands. His gaze was fixed on hers and the look in his eyes gave her an odd tingle. Were the results of the study she was talking about really that fascinating?

It was a relief when their food arrived but, a short time later, Emilia realised she might have been more wary of trying this new restaurant if she'd also known that they specialised in platters of food for sharing and that cutlery was optional. There was something rather intimate in reaching for a delicious taste of twice-fried crispy potato skin or tiny, melt-in-the-mouth pulled beef slider when your hand could brush that of the person you were sharing the meal with. They had finger bowls that came with a tray of barbecued ribs to clean sticky fingers so they both managed to eat all they desired without picking up a fork.

More than all they desired, in fact.

'I'm stuffed,' Emilia finally announced.

'Me, too. But I'm still going to eat that last rib. Unless you'd like it?'

She shook her head. 'I would explode. It wouldn't be pretty.'

Dom grinned and then closed his eyes as he tore into the succulent meat. 'I think this might be the best dinner I've ever had,' he said as he discarded the bone.

'It helps to have not eaten all day. They say that hunger is the best condiment for anything.' Emilia couldn't take her eyes off Dom's face. The sweep of those dark, dark lashes on his cheeks beneath that still rumpled hair and the way his lips curled up at the corners even though they looked completely relaxed…

He'd look like this when he was asleep, wouldn't he? In bed…

Emilia was sure she almost visibly jumped as Dom's eyes opened again.

'What? Have I got something on my face?'

'Ah…actually, yes…' Emilia found what she hoped was a casual smile. 'Barbecue sauce, probably.'

'Oh…' Dom picked up his napkin and wiped his mouth. 'Is it gone?'

'Mmm…'

'You've got some as well.' But Dom was reaching across the table as he spoke so Emilia didn't have a chance to pick up her own napkin. He wiped the bottom of her cheek, right at the corner of her mouth, with the back of his thumb. 'There you go. All gone.'

Emilia couldn't say anything. That touch, so close to her lips, had stolen her breath completely. Maybe she was looking a little strange, as well, because Dom was staring at her and she'd never seen quite that expression on his face before.

'What?' she finally managed. 'There's more sauce?'

He shook his head. Looked away but then back to catch her gaze. The tone of his voice was curiously hesitant.

'I was just wondering,' he murmured.

'Wondering what?'

'Why you're still single. You're beautiful, Emmy...'

Emilia swallowed hard. Again, she was lost for words. She couldn't look away from those dark eyes, either. It felt like she could fall into them.

And drown...

'Not only that, you're damn good at what you do. And you're independent and ambitious and successful and— What?' Dom broke off. 'Why are you shaking your head like that?'

'You're answering your own question,' Emilia said. 'About why I'm single? It's not necessarily a good thing for a woman to be ambitious and successful.'

Dom's breath came out in a disbelieving huff.

'It's true,' she insisted. 'It's precisely why my last relationship didn't work out. He— Chandler—got more and more resentful of my achievements. When I got promoted over him, that was the end…' She couldn't bring herself to tell him what else Chandler had said—that no man would ever want to be with someone like her. Someone who had to prove herself to be better all the time by putting someone else down. A…ballbreaker.

But it seemed like she didn't need to tell him the worst of it. His gaze had already darkened noticeably.

'He was an idiot,' he growled. 'And a *bastardo*.'

The word didn't need translating. And the

vehemence with which he was taking her side made the corners of Emilia's mouth curl up.

'I don't even understand,' he continued. 'We fought like…do you say tooth and nail? Or cats and dogs perhaps, to be the best at medical school, didn't we?' He didn't wait for her response. 'I hated it when you beat me but…you know what?'

'What?'

'I was proud of you, too, in the end. I hated losing but, at the same time, I was so happy that you were winning because you deserved to win.' His mouth twitched. 'Not that I would have ever told you that, of course.'

Oh… He'd been proud of her, back then, when she'd won a race to first place? He'd hidden it well, that was for sure, but knowing that he'd felt like that was melting something inside Emilia. It also made complete sense because she'd had the same sort of reaction when he'd won, hadn't she? She'd decided it was simply grudging admiration but perhaps she'd never recognised it for what it had actually been.

'You can't ever be with someone like that again,' Dom said softly. 'It's hard enough to fight for what you need to achieve without someone pulling you down.'

Emilia nodded slowly. 'That's so true. I already knew that I had to rely on myself and believe in my ambition. I'll never let anybody else pull me down. I'm happier on my own, anyway.'

'Even then, it can be hard.' Dom's breath came out in a sigh. 'I've had to fight, too. I feel like I'm still fighting but maybe now it's against myself instead of my father. A battle between what I want to do and what I have to do.'

Emilia swallowed hard. She should break this eye contact but she couldn't. What she wanted more than anything, in this moment, was to help Dom. To give him a gift as meaningful as the one he'd just given her, in telling her that she was special enough for him to have been proud of her. And, if he was going to believe her, he needed to see how genuine she was, so she held his gaze.

'There must be a way you can be true to yourself and still do your duty,' she said quietly. 'You're too good a doctor to walk away from your career. You still have lives to save and…and maybe continuing your work is something that you need to save what's so important in your own life.' She took a deep breath. 'I read about Isola Verde. About the wonderful new hospital that's been built there.'

Dom nodded. 'That's Giada's doing,' he told her. 'Despite how young she is, she has a passion for our country and she wanted the best health care to be available for our people.'

'Couldn't you work there? Even if it was only part-time? Find a compromise between what you have to do and what you want to do?'

This time Dom shook his head. 'I don't do compromise,' he said. 'It has to be all or nothing for me. If I choose to do something, I will give it my whole heart and soul. My everything. There can be no half measures. When I commit, that's for ever.'

Wow... Emilia let her breath out very slowly. The sincerity in those words. The passion that they advertised. She could imagine him being this genuine when he committed to a woman he loved. Whoever she turned out to be, Emilia hoped she would know that she was the luckiest woman on earth...

It was Dom who broke the eye contact. And, as if he realised that the atmosphere was getting too heavy, he cleared his throat.

'Speaking of Giada, she tells me that she's going to be back in time to come to the fundraising gala. So is Lucas, apparently. I must remember to get some more tickets for them tomorrow. Are you coming, Emmy?'

'No. I usually work during events like that, so other people get to go. Like I always work on Christmas Day. Not that they needed any extras on the night of gala this time, though.'

'You don't like dressing up?' Dom's glance grazed hers again. 'Now that I come to think of it, I don't think I've ever seen you wearing a dress.'

Emilia shrugged. 'I don't wear them often. And I don't own a cocktail dress, let alone a ballgown.'

'So buy one. Or rent one?'

'Why would I do that?'

Dom had her pinned with his gaze again. 'So that you can come to the gala with me, of course.'

Emilia's jaw sagged. 'Are you asking me out on a *date*?'

That flicker in his gaze...it almost looked

like...*desire*? Oh, dear Lord...that knot in her gut hadn't just tightened. It felt like it might be disintegrating in a small explosion that was sending waves of sensation to parts of her body that had been peacefully shut away for a long time now.

But Dom was smiling now. 'I'm asking you as a friend,' he told her. 'My best friend. Maybe the only one who'll ever know me for just who I really am. In here...' He touched his chest in that gesture that was becoming so familiar but Emilia could see the muscles in her throat move at the same time, as he swallowed carefully.

They did have something totally unique between them.

Something that couldn't last.

But, right now...it felt like someone was waving a magic wand. Creating a snippet of a fairy tale that cast Emilia Featherstone in a Cinderella role. She was being offered the chance of going to the ball and she already knew that she would be dancing with a prince...

It was such a fantasy that it made her smile. If she was someone who cried, she might well have been fighting back tears right now but, instead, she just smiled more—although the edges of that smile felt a bit wobbly.

'I'd love to come,' she said.

CHAPTER SIX

THE CHRISTMAS CHARITY fundraising gala was still days away but Emilia had already had far too much time to think about it.

To think about Domenico.

Not that she'd seen much of him since the night they'd had dinner together. Even when their schedules could have allowed them to meet for a run in the park, the weather had been cold and wet enough to prevent that happening. There'd even been sleet one day and weather forecasts were predicting snow before Christmas. Trauma team callouts had been few and far between as well and Emilia had missed two of them because she'd been in Theatre and the cases had been complicated enough not to be able to let her senior resident take over. Their paths had crossed yesterday in the ICU when Emilia had been making one of her regular visits to follow the progress of Roberto's recovery from his leg injury but that had been a strictly professional interaction. Until, that was, Dom had tilted his head and lowered his voice as if he was saying something about the notes Emilia had made in Roberto's patient file that he didn't want anybody else to hear.

'Got that dress yet?' he'd murmured.

Emilia had shaken her head. 'Haven't had time to go shopping,' she said quietly. 'And I'm not really sure I want to go. I don't even know how to dance.'

The amused glint in Dom's eyes had told her that he thought he knew exactly what was bothering her—that, like him perhaps, she hated doing something in public unless she knew she could do it very, very well.

'You're coming,' he'd said softly. 'You're going to show the world that you're capable of doing anything, Dr Featherstone.' His lips twitched. 'Even wearing a dress...'

So, here she was. In one of Seattle's largest department stores, in the area devoted to evening dresses and ballgowns. With spacious changing rooms and a huge, gilt-framed mirror for anyone who wanted to come out of the private cubicles to get the full effect of the gown they were trying on.

'Do you need some help in there?'

'No… I'm good. I don't think I like this, though.'

'Come out and look in the big mirror. It can make a difference.'

But the classic 'little black dress' Emilia was trying didn't look any better from a distance, even when she held her hair up to pretend she had a sophisticated evening updo to go with it. The black fabric made her skin look far too pale and there was rather too much of it on show with that short skirt length.

'It makes me look like a member of the Addams family,' she sighed. 'Or like I'm on my way to a Hollywood funeral. It's not right for a Christmas ball, is it?'

'Hmm…' The grey-haired senior shop assistant—Margie, according to her name badge—pursed her lips as the gaze she had focussed on Emilia became thoughtful. 'It's not the Seattle General Christmas gala that you're going to, is it?'

'It is.'

'Lucky you. That's the most A-list party

we get around these parts. Where's it being held this year?'

'At the Polar Club Hotel, I believe.'

'Oh…' The older woman actually clasped her hands in awe. 'I've been in there. That room with the dome ceiling and the chandeliers is incredible…' She let her breath out in a long sigh. That thoughtful expression had given way to something more like determination. 'Right… Take that dress off, love. I've got something else I think you definitely have to try on.'

Emilia went back into the small changing room and it was a relief to peel the black dress from her body. Imagine what Dom would have thought if she'd turned up with her legs on display like that? Would she have seen that spark of whatever it was she'd seen the other night rekindled in his gaze? That mutual physical awareness that had launched shafts of desire, the aftermath of which was still powerful enough to be disturbing.

Did she *want* to see that?

Oh, man… For a long moment, Emilia held the dress against her bare midriff as she felt the now familiar spiral of sensations deep within. Fragments of many conversations

she'd had with herself in the last few days—
mostly in that quiet space of sleepless hours
when it wasn't possible to distract yourself—
were swirling in her head again now.

She'd always known that Domenico di
Rossi was dangerous. Right from that first
moment she'd seen his effect on the women
around him at medical school. It had been
at that moment that she'd vowed to ignore
him on a personal level because nothing was
going to distract her from her dream of becoming a doctor and escaping every dark
thing her life had included so far.

Those reasons were no longer valid, however. Emilia had long since arrived at where
she'd dreamed of being. She'd escaped her
past to the extent that the only contact with
anybody from her early life was the annual
Christmas card she sent to Mrs Delaney—the
person who'd encouraged her to believe that
she could escape. What would her eleventh-
grade teacher think of her now, she wondered,
if she could see her getting ready to try on
a ballgown to wear to attend one of Seattle's
most glittering nights of the year in the prestigious and historic Polar Club Hotel?

No…any danger that Dom represented now

had nothing to do with her ambitions. As her sleepless nights had forced Emilia to pick at the knot of emotions that were building and try to understand what was going on, she recognised that the danger now was that she was playing with fire. That what was going on here had the potential to hurt her enough to cause some lasting damage.

She cared about Dom. She had done for far longer than she'd ever realised. Their rivalry and their banter had been protection and a very effective disguise for the significance their connection had always had the potential to have. Had she really thought that these new feelings were nothing like having a crush on someone or falling in love? Maybe if she'd faced this earlier, she could have stopped herself before she'd travelled too far down that path of falling in love but it felt like she'd passed the point of no return now. She couldn't stop thinking about him. Couldn't stop her body from letting her know just how much it wanted to be a whole lot closer to the man.

How many girls at medical school had felt like this about Dom? The lucky ones had enjoyed a brief time in his life and presumably in his bed but, even back then, she'd been aware of a curious level of control on Dom's part. Despite his popularity and charm, he'd always kept an emotional distance and ended relationships before they became anything serious. She understood why now. Dom couldn't afford to fall in love with just anyone, could he? Not when the woman he chose to share his life would eventually become the Queen of his country?

At least Emilia had an advantage that none of those girls had had, because she knew that the path of falling in love with Domenico di Rossi had that dead end. And thank goodness Dom had no idea how she felt. She'd told him she was happy on her own and it was true. She *was* happy on her own. She certainly wasn't about to invent any fantasies based on a future with him because she knew what was coming and that it was quite possible that Dom would vanish from her life before Christmas, which wasn't that far away. There were children all over the world who had started counting down how many sleeps until then. Waiting for the magic to happen.

'Here I am…' Margie the shop assistant sounded breathless. 'Sorry to take so long.

This dress had been put out the back. It's actually from the season before last but…it's special…and, as a bonus, we'll be able to give you a great discount on it.'

Emilia opened the door of her changing area and actually laughed aloud. 'It's *red*. Haven't you noticed my hair?'

'Pfft… Who listens to old-fashioned rules like that these days? For goodness sake, some girls have blue or green hair now. Nobody's making rules about what colours they're allowed or not allowed to wear, are they?'

Emilia couldn't argue with that. And Margie was looking so excited, she had to humour her by trying on the dress. Her legs certainly weren't visible under the mass of floor length ripples of silk and the embroidered and beaded bodice with its low, sweetheart neckline fitted like a glove as it got zipped up. With a built-in bra there was nothing to detract from the delicate, lace straps that put the colour right beside the loose waves of Emilia's hair.

And, if anything, this shade of scarlet was like a celebration of her hair colour rather than anything that clashed horribly.

'Come out and look in the big mirror again,' Margie urged.

Emilia could feel the skirt rippling around her legs as she moved. When she stepped up to look at herself in the mirror, she instinctively smoothed her hands over her hips, where the dress clung before exploding into what felt like miles of fabric that was so fine it still hung close to her body. And maybe it was the feel of her hands on silk that was like a second skin that started the fairy dust. That made her imagine so clearly how it would feel if it was Dom's hands on her hips instead of her own. The thought took her breath away completely.

She didn't need to wait for any form of Christmas magic because she had her own magic happening right now.

A red Cinderella ballgown to wear.

A prince waiting to dance with her.

'Oh, love...' Margie's voice was no more than a whisper. 'Don't you look like a princess?'

That should have added to the fairy dust but, instead, Emilia was aware of a wash of something like panic. She kept her gaze on her reflection but pressed her fingers against her lips. What did she think she was doing—planning to go out with a prince for the evening? What if there were paparazzi around and photos came out everywhere and people found out where she'd come from and Dom ended up being embarrassed by her?

Emilia could feel that odd prickle at the back of her eyes again. Why was her body suddenly remembering how to form tears? If she wasn't careful, they might escape one of these days and what would that do for the tough, confident image she'd cultivated so well for so long? The tears weren't going to fall this time but they did smudge her reflection in the mirror enough to make it dream-like.

And that's all this was. A small step out of real life for a very limited amount of time. A once-in-a-lifetime opportunity, in fact, because Dom's identity couldn't stay secret for ever. But it was still secret now and that meant there wouldn't be any paparazzi. The only thing that would shock anybody from Seattle General would be that she and Dom were attending a social event together instead of baiting each other or competing in some way.

They weren't to know how much further from real life Emilia's evening out was. How she really felt about Dom. Or that she was still a little dubious about wearing this colour for the first time in her life. She'd always been told to never wear red. Along with being told that she'd never amount to anything. That she'd end up just like her no-good mother.

She could hear a dismissive huff at the back of her mind and it sounded a lot like Mrs Delaney. She could even imagine exactly what her beloved teacher might say if she was standing here beside her.

You've already proved all those small-minded people wrong so why on earth would you think you can't wear red? You can do anything you want, Emilia Featherstone. Be whoever you want. Get out there and celebrate, my girl. Believe in yourself. Be proud of yourself...

Dom had told her she was capable of doing anything. He wanted to see her wearing a dress. It had to be *this* dress because even if it was an imagined conversation with Mrs Delaney, her words rang true.

Emilia *was* proud of herself.

And she wanted Dom to be proud of her again as well—the way he said he had been when she'd shown that she could beat him academically. Maybe this could be an escape from real life for him, too—before he had to face the unimaginable responsibilities of ruling a country. A small fantasy that he would remember—a magic night together with her—for many years after he was gone. One that she, Emilia, suspected she would be remembering for the rest of her life.

She swallowed hard but then turned to smile brightly at Margie. 'This dress is perfect,' she said. 'Just the colour for Christmas.'

The Northern Star Dome Room of the Polar Club Hotel was a colourful scene—impressive even for someone who'd grown up being a part of lavish royal events. The glittering chandelier, the rococo motifs, the massive leaded, stained glass, domed ceiling that was subtly illuminated in festive shades of red and green made a wonderful backdrop for tables that had crisp, white linen cloths, floral decorations and sparkling silverware and crystal.

The colour that was impressing Dom the most, however, was the bright hue of Emilia's gorgeous red dress. It wasn't just the dress, either. The pale skin of her bare arms and shoulders seemed to have been dusted with some kind of shimmery powder. Her make-up was flawless but Dom liked that it was still natural enough for her distinctive freckles to show through. That fiery hair of hers had been cleverly looped up into a sort of bun although curly strands had been left to float down her neck and softly frame her face. There were even tiny red jewelled flowers that were somehow wound into her hair and sparkled every time she moved her head.

Emilia wasn't just a very attractive woman. *Dio bono...* She was *stunning...*

And she was his partner for the evening. Dom normally kept as low a profile as possible at any events like this, where photographers were keen to get shots for the social pages of local publications but tonight he didn't care. It wasn't just that his identity was not going to stay secret for much longer, given that he would be returning to rule Isola Verde very soon, it was that he was proud to be Emilia's partner. Proud of her, doing something that he suspected was well out of her comfort zone. Proud of how beautiful she was, as well. He wanted to show her off to the world.

And this small corner of the world was most definitely looking astonished that he and Emilia had apparently come as partners when they were always giving each other such a hard time at work. Well…wait until they saw them dancing together later, Dom thought, as he chose a delicious looking risotto ball from the tray of hors-d'oeuvres a waiter was offering on a silver tray. As long as Emilia allowed him to lead her, of course, and didn't decide it was some sort of competition that she needed to win. Dom knew that if she could suppress her desire to be the best, for once, he could make her look fabulous on the dance floor. He was actually looking forward to that part of the evening with a surprisingly delicious anticipation.

In the meantime, he had to wonder why Ayanna Franklin was staring at him with such concentration. A quirk of his eyebrow had her apologising instantly.

'Sorry… I was just wondering if you liked that risotto ball.'

'It was delicious.'

'And have you tried the smoked salmon? Or the chicken satay skewers?'

'I've tried the chicken skewers,' Emilia told Ayanna. 'They're delicious, too.'

'Oh…thank goodness for that.' Ayanna let out a relieved breath. 'I haven't had time to try them myself yet. There's a lot to do to make sure an event this size goes well.'

'Relax,' Emilia told her. 'Enjoy yourself. You've done a wonderful job of organising this gala—I'm so impressed.'

'Me too,' Dom said, turning his head as he noticed his father's neurosurgeon coming towards them. 'Hi, Max… We're just saying what an amazing job Ayanna's done with the decorations and catering for tonight.'

Max Granger's nod was polite but Ayanna didn't look reassured by either Dom's praise or Max's agreement. If anything, she was looking even more tense.

'Excuse me… I'd better go and check up on how things are going in the kitchens.'

Ayanna's green dress vanished amongst the crowd as Dom let his gaze scan the room.

'I wonder if Giada's here yet?'

'She is,' Max told him, and then lowered his voice. 'I've spoken to her and told her

what I told you earlier today—that if…ah…
Mr Baresi's condition continues to improve
we can look at going ahead with his original surgery very soon. Maybe as soon as the
planned date of the fifteenth. I should have a
better idea after the scan that's booked in for
first thing tomorrow.'

Dom acknowledged the information with
no more than a single nod. 'I'll see her soon
enough,' he murmured. 'I believe we're seated
at the same table for dinner and it looks as
though they're getting ready to serve the first
course.'

Max turned to move away but then looked
back. 'Don't miss the dessert,' he told them.
'It's something very special. Worth all the effort it took to find.'

Emilia watched him walk away. 'I wonder
how he knows that?' she said. 'I thought the
food tonight was Ayanna's responsibility.'

'One of them,' Dom agreed. 'She's had
rather a lot of responsibility lately what with
trying to ensure that information that needs
to stay private stays that way. And part of that
is the reason why Max is here, of course. I
believe she's been working closely with him.'

'Well, I hope she gets to enjoy tonight. It

would be unfair if it's just stressful for her. Oh…look…there's Lucas. I haven't seen him since the day of the accident.'

'No…' Dom was delighted to see his best friend again. And his sister, who was approaching with Lucas, although he couldn't advertise their relationship by anything as personal as a hug. He was smiling warmly as he greeted her, however.

'You're looking good, Gigi.'

Better than good, he thought. It was more than the lovely, purple dress she was wearing, with the sparkly top that left one shoulder bare. Or the earrings that looked as if they were part of the royal family's famous collection of rare jewels. His sister probably didn't need the accessories to make her look so good because she was almost glowing.

'You look like you've caught a nice bit of sunshine,' he added.

Giada was smiling back at him. 'Hard not to in Isola Verde,' she said. 'Even in winter.'

'It's the most beautiful place,' Lucas agreed. He was looking at Giada as he spoke but then looked back to catch Dom's raised eyebrow.

'Or so Gigi's told me,' he added hurriedly.

Dom blinked this time. There weren't that many people who got to call the Crown Princess of Isola Verde by her pet name.

'Your dress is beautiful,' Emilia was saying to Giada.

'So is yours. That red is spectacular.' Giada slid a sideways look at her brother and then back at Emilia, clearly wondering what their connection was. 'You work together, yes? Didn't I see you in the ER on the day of the accident?'

'Yes, but we only work together sometimes. I'm a trauma surgeon with the orthopaedic department at Seattle General.'

'We went to medical school together,' Dom put in. 'We're old friends, Gigi, that's all.'

The idea of even being 'old friends' would have seemed presumptuous just a few weeks ago, but things between them had changed so much that the idea that someone would think they were actually a couple didn't seem far-fetched at all. The idea was not unpleasant, either. Impossible, of course, but what man wouldn't want to follow through on an attraction that had been taken to an entirely new level this evening?

'Oh…' Giada's response was drawn out

just enough to suggest she didn't quite believe that. The glance she shared with Lucas suggested that they had a silent conversation thing going on which made Dom wonder about connections between people but Giada turned away before he could ask any leading questions and he was distracted by her profile. His sister wasn't just looking good because of the sunshine she'd been enjoying, it looked as though she'd made the most of the wonderful Italian food while she'd been at home. Or maybe it was just the cut of her dress that was making the most of her curves. Either way, it certainly wasn't something Dom was going to mention.

Between courses, people were changing places or walking amongst the tables to chat with friends and toast what they hoped was going to be a record-breaking fundraising event.

'Those tickets were well worth that hefty price tag,' one of Seattle General's obstetricians said to Dom and Emilia. 'This place is amazing. And the food… I can't wait for the dessert I saw on the menu. I have no idea what a London Fog Cake could be but I suspect I might have to start my New Year's diet before Christmas at this rate.'

'It's all delicious,' Emilia agreed. 'That salad we started with…mmm… What was it called again?'

'Caprese,' Dom said. 'It's an Italian classic.'

'Ah…' The obstetrician smiled at Dom. 'That would be right up your alley, then. You've got Italian heritage, haven't you?'

'It's been a while since I've been there.' Dom didn't want to discuss his heritage and he was well-practised in deflecting awkward questions. 'I'm more than half American now, I reckon. I didn't realise that Seattle had a gem like this amongst its hotels, though. Do you know anything about its history?'

'Not much. I do know it's just over a hundred years old because they had some centenary celebrations not that long ago.'

Another Seattle General specialist stepped close to join the conversation. 'I heard a story that the name came from a group of men who'd struck it rich in the Yukon gold rush and they formed a group and called it the Polar Club.'

'Makes sense,' Emilia put in. 'The Yukon's on the border with Alaska, isn't it? With a coast on the Arctic Ocean? That must have been pretty cold…'

Dom excused himself to visit the restrooms and, by the time he returned, he saw that dessert was being served. Waiters were carrying silver trays with the most extraordinary looking cakes on top. With the smoky looking, streaked grey icing on the cakes, it was obvious where that unusual name had come from.

He stepped back to let a waiter walk past and found his steps slowing to a halt as he watched and listened for a moment. All around him he could hear animated conversation and laughter and cries of admiration as each table's dessert was served. He could also hear the music from the small, live band, who'd been playing mostly classical music so far but seemed to be changing to popular music now, perhaps as a prelude to encouraging people to use the dance floor. It was still a brightly coloured, happy scene but right now, Dom didn't feel a part of it at all.

Maybe it was because his sister was here, having just returned from Isola Verde and it was a reminder of how his life was about to be tipped upside down and that disturbing feeling had been dramatically heightened by the salad they'd been served this evening. A Caprese, for heaven's sake. Tomatoes and mozzarella cheese and basil with a delicious olive oil that could have come straight from his homeland. Every bite had been full of the flavour of his former life—a life he was about to reluctantly step back into.

Most of the people in this spectacular ballroom were his colleagues. People who shared his passion for medicine and were as proud as he was of working in such a prestigious hospital. Dom's gaze travelled back to the table nearest the dance floor. To the splash of vivid red that was Emilia's dress. Of all the people here, she was the one who understood the most. Who was his soul mate as far as how important their careers were to who *they* actually were. The only other person he knew who'd needed to escape their background to be who they really were.

Dom didn't want things to change but it was happening. With what Max had told him this evening, that process of change could be about to speed up. Whatever the outcome of his father's next surgery, they would have to share the news and that would be the moment that Domenico di Rossi would have to

become Domenico Baresi again. When he'd
have to walk away from the life he loved so
much here. From the people he loved working with.

From Emilia…

Another waiter went past where Dom was
standing, this time carrying a tray of full
champagne flutes. Dom reached out to accept the offer of a glass.

He still had tonight, he told himself, as he
took a long sip and then another of the champagne. And maybe this was going to be his
last chance to cling to everything he loved
about this life, so he'd better make the most
of it, hadn't he?

Another long sip emptied his glass and another waiter took it from his hand as Dom
walked back to his table.

To Emmy…

Dessert could wait, as far as he was concerned, anyway. If he was to make the most
of what time he had left and not think about
what was coming he had the best distraction
of all waiting for him. Watching him walk
towards her with a smile on her face, in fact.
He held his hand out as he reached the table.

'Come and dance with me,' he invited.

CHAPTER SEVEN

YES...

   No...

Time seemed to stop for a long, long moment as Emilia stared at Dom's outstretched hand.

She'd noticed him off to one side of the ballroom in the last few minutes, standing alone as he drank a glass of champagne. She'd been instantly aware of him as soon as he'd started moving back towards their table, too, and it had taken quite some effort not to watch every step he took.

Almost any man could look good in a formal, black tie outfit but Dom looked as though he'd been born to wear a superbly cut tuxedo and matching trousers, the snowy white shirt with pin tucks, hidden buttons and the flash of gold cufflinks and, of course, the black silk bow tie.

But he *had* been born to wear it, hadn't he? Born to shine at events just like this charity gala, as part of a royal family which was pretty much as A-list as anyone could ever be. Emilia had no doubts at all that Dom would know how to dance very well. Infinitely better than she could hope to, despite the secret practice in the privacy of her apartment, with the help of online tutorials that she'd made time for ever since she'd accepted his invitation to be his partner tonight.

Which was why her brain had suddenly become a battleground, with the two sides slugging it out so fast, nobody would guess what was going on behind her smile as Dom put out his hand.

Yes…one side wanted nothing more than to be close enough to touch this man. To be touched *by* him… To feel his hands on the silk of her dress the way her own hands had been when she'd first tried it on. She had to find out if that sensation was anything like as breathtaking as it had been in her imagination, not only when she'd put this astonishing dress on that first time, but every time she'd seen it hanging in the corner of her bedroom since then.

But no… The other side was putting up a valiant opposition. Emilia had known there would be dancing involved but she'd imagined that she'd be amongst enough people on a crowded dance floor that it wouldn't matter that she didn't really know how to dance. This invitation had come too early in the evening and there were only a few couples who were already on the polished wooden floor in front of the band which meant that Emilia would be being watched by a large number of people. Many of her colleagues had already been unable to hide their surprise that she was here with Dom in the first place so she could be sure that more than a few jaws would be dropping to see them dancing together.

This was a challenge, for sure.

But this was also Dom and when had she ever backed down from any kind of challenge he'd presented?

This might be a good time to make an exception and back down, that voice in her head warned. She might be in danger of making a complete fool of herself. Or worse, taking herself back to the time in her life when being in a spotlight had been far worse than simply embarrassing. When it had meant that she was being taken to a new family because her current foster parents no longer wanted such a difficult child. Or that she was being sent to the principal's office because she was in trouble. Again. Even recently, the spotlight of her professional success had come with the pain of a failed relationship.

With that kind of background, mustering a defensive barrier was something that could be done in the blink of an eye but Emilia had never had to put that barrier up in the face of something so strong on the other side—a desire that was powerful enough to be sweeping anything else aside. Not only that, she was wearing the red dress. Her Cinderella dress. The one that told her that she could be anyone she wanted to be.

And, right now, Emilia wanted to be the person who was taking hold of Dom's hand. The woman that was about to be held in his arms. A princess for just a blink of time. She wanted it so much that her hand was reaching out to touch his even before she could consciously choose to shut down the protest in her head. It was quite possible that no one had noticed the tiny hesitation she'd had in taking Dom's hand but he'd obviously seen something in her eyes.

Thankfully, he couldn't possibly know why that internal battle had been so convincingly won but he must have guessed that her inner turmoil was due to a fear of some kind of failure, because, as he took her in his arms moments later, he put his mouth close to Emilia's ear and said a few words that changed everything.

'Trust me, Emmy… I've got this…'

His voice tickled her ear. One of his hands was covering hers and the other was against the small of her back and she could feel the heat of it, as though the silk of her dress had evaporated. And his touch was everything she'd imagined it might be. And more… Emilia could feel it in every cell of her body and she was melting. Muscles that had been poised for a physical challenge were relaxing and she even closed her eyes as she felt the power in Dom's hands. Guiding her. Holding her. Making a promise that he was not going to let her fall.

Except she was. As the sweet notes of Celine Dion's 'Think Twice' created the ocean of sound they were floating on, Emilia could feel herself falling. She'd been halfway in love with Dom before this and had been afraid that going any further could be dangerous but there was no stopping what was happening here.

This feeling of complete trust was something she'd never experienced before and there was more there as well. She was feeling protected. Cared for. Respected.

As she responded to the push and pull of his arms, Dom turned her away from him and then twirled her under his arm before drawing her close again. She caught a glimpse of his face, of the gleam in those dark eyes that told her she was doing much better than he might have expected.

That he was proud of her...?

That did it. Emilia hit the bottom of wherever that fall had been taking her and...it didn't hurt a bit. Quite the opposite. She'd never felt this happy in her life. And maybe this would be the only time in her life that she would ever feel this happy so she was going to hang onto every single second of it for as long as it lasted.

Oh, mio Dio...

The feel of this woman in his arms...

Emilia was perfectly capable of fighting as hard as it took to try and prove that she was the best at anything she attempted but she must have instinctively known that that would have been the worst approach to dancing. That what she had to do was trust enough to let someone lead her. She had to listen to what his body and hands were telling her and not to argue back—to simply follow where he led. And that was exactly what she was doing.

She was trusting him…

It was enough to make Dom's heart feel full to bursting because he knew that this wasn't a small thing for Emilia. After seeing that flash of something that could have even been fear in her eyes when he'd invited her onto the dance floor, he wouldn't have been at all surprised if she'd found an excuse to stay seated at their table, but here she was, melting in his arms when he held her close but with exactly the tension that was needed when he wanted to turn and spin her to show her off.

A spin that he could keep complete control of, unlike the way his life was beginning to turn in on itself. At least almost nobody here knew anything about how his life was about to change. They knew him only as a doctor who was striving—and succeeding—in being at the top of his challenging field of emergency medicine. The way Emilia had known him only as a fellow medical student and now her colleague until he'd dropped that bombshell and revealed his true identity.

This wasn't the first time that Dom realised that his relationship with Emilia was the only one he would ever be able to trust as being completely genuine. She was also inextricably woven into the world he'd fought so hard to join.

She was one of the most memorable parts of all those years at medical school.

She was a part of his work that he loved the most, when he was faced with the huge challenges of dealing with major trauma.

Even for just those two reasons, she was—and always would be—a part of *him*.

It was just as well that his instincts had warned him to stay away from personal involvement with her all those years ago because it was blatantly obvious to him at this moment that, in another world, he would have fallen in love with Emilia.

He still could…

And he certainly wasn't helping anything

by discovering the delicious curves of her body with his hand shaping her waist and hip beneath the slippery fabric of that amazing dress. By being close enough to catch the scent of her skin and to feel the touch of her hand inside his. Most of all, to be aware of just how much she was trusting him.

If only he was the kind of prince who belonged in a fairy tale and had a fairy godmother who could wave a magic wand to make any obstacles melt away. He would not only be more than happy to give up his career to become King, but Emilia would also walk away from the job that was the most important thing in her life so that she could be by his side for ever.

It was never going to work, of course, but… just for a little while, Dom could pretend, couldn't he?

That he wasn't a prince. That his life wasn't going to change so completely he was sure he would never be truly happy again. He could cling to the things he loved for a little longer. It was only one night. A few magical hours where he could hold the most beautiful woman in the world in his arms and they could lose themselves in this romantic music and a dream or two of what might have been.

The rest of Seattle General's fundraising charity gala went past in a blur for Emilia. There were snatches of conversation she was never going to remember, a glass or two of champagne that fizzed and evaporated on her tongue almost instantly and a swirl of colours and music that was the dance floor she found herself on again and again and almost always with Dom. The one thing that Emilia was sure of, as she finally went outside to find a taxi, was that the only word that could ever sum up what this evening had been like was: *magic*.

And it seemed that the fairy tale hadn't quite ended.

The tall man in the tuxedo who had flagged down a taxi and was now holding the back door open for her was none other than her Prince. Domenico di Rossi.

'Jump in,' he told her. 'But do you mind if I share?'

Of course she didn't. What could be a better ending to such a magical evening than being in the back seat of a taxi beside Dom, with the cloud of red silk spilling onto his dark suit and the strobe effect of the street lights overhead making his eyes sparkle as she caught his gaze.

The taxi stopped for a red light, somewhere very close to the Space Needle and Emilia had to tilt her head to gaze up and admire the elegant structure that held what looked like a spaceship with all its lights on. Dom had done exactly the same thing and then, as if they couldn't resist the magnetic pull, they both turned their heads enough to look at each other.

For the second time in the space of one evening, time stopped for Emilia. But this was way bigger than looking at Dom's outstretched hand and the internal battle that it had generated.

There was no battle here. Nothing could break a connection that felt powerful enough to tilt the world's axis. Nothing was going to interfere with the inevitability that this was going to happen.

This…kiss…

A physical touch that Emilia hadn't realised she'd been waiting for forever. A touch that made her understand exactly what had always been missing from her life—this connection with another human. This feeling that she was wanted. Needed. Loved…?

The jerk of the taxi moving away on the green light wasn't enough for that kiss to be broken. It took the taxi driver's loud clearing of his throat when the taxi had stopped again a short time later for Emilia and Dom to finally break apart.

'This is the first stop,' the driver said. 'Who's getting out here?'

'I am.' Dom handed some bills to the driver and opened the door. He stepped out, then leaned down so that he could catch Emilia's gaze again. He wasn't smiling but there was a warmth in his eyes that made it impossible to look away and Emilia's senses were suddenly so heightened that it didn't matter that his words were no more than a murmur against the background of traffic noise. She could hear what he said, as he held out his hand to her for the second time that evening, as clearly as if his lips had been brushing her ear.

'Come with me?'

Oh…

Everything was spinning. A kaleidoscope

of the entire evening. The gorgeous ballroom, the swish of a dress that Emilia was going to keep for ever, the wonderful food, the delicious champagne, the beautiful dresses of all the women and the music that had kept her dancing all night. The whole—incredible—fairy tale and the man who had been at the centre of everything was inviting her to make it last a little longer.

He'd just kissed her senseless and now he wanted more.

And, dear Lord, so did Emilia.

She wanted everything. She wanted it so much that she didn't hesitate for more than a heartbeat and she knew, by the way Dom's hand closed around her own, that she'd made the only choice she could have made.

Like that kiss, it felt like Emilia had been waiting her whole life for this…

He'd always known it was there, hadn't he?

And he'd been right to be afraid of it.

This…*connection*…

This feeling that *this* person, and only this person, could touch your soul, as much as your body, and make it feel like you'd…come home. That you'd finally found the place you truly belonged.

Dom had to kiss Emilia again, the moment the elevator doors closed behind them, because he couldn't wait until they reached the privacy of his apartment to find out if that kiss in the taxi had actually been what it had seemed to be, or if it had simply been his imagination, the combination of an evening full of pleasure or perhaps the frustration of having waited for so many years to kiss Emilia Featherstone that had created nothing short of a magic spell. Would kissing her now be like kissing any other attractive woman? He'd certainly had enough practice to be able to make that judgement.

Unbelievably, this second kiss was even more astonishing. Reaching the penthouse level of this apartment block, the elevator doors slid open, stayed open and then closed again without either of them noticing. The touch and taste of her lips, the seductive dance of her tongue was driving any conscious thought from Dom's mind. It was only the need for a little more oxygen that made him finally pull back, to find Emilia looking just as stunned as he was feeling.

Her lips were still parted a little and her eyes glazed by desire and the only thing Dom wanted to do was to kiss her again. To kiss every inch of her body, in fact, and he certainly couldn't do that in this elevator which seemed to have stopped. Was it stuck? He pushed the button to open the doors to find that they had already arrived at his floor and that he had absolutely no concept of how much time had passed during that kiss.

Oh, *sì*… He hadn't been wrong that first time he'd laid eyes on Emilia back at medical school. When he'd known instantly that it would be dangerous to get close to her in any personal way. As he held his apartment door open for her and she went past him with a swish of silk and a lingering upward glance, Dom could remember vividly that first sight of this woman. Those blue, blue eyes that made him think of the sea that surrounded Isola Verde. The glorious glint of so many different shades of red in that magnificent hair, including the copper that was reflected in the freckles that dusted her pale skin.

Distraction…
Destruction…
He'd put up the fences right there and

then. Had mentally painted the word 'Danger' across the palings in the same shade of red as Emilia's dress was tonight. Moments after shoving his door shut behind him with his foot, Dom's hands were on the smooth silk of that dress again. Emilia was standing on tiptoe, her arms around his neck as he kissed her yet again. Dom had found the zip that was falling open beneath his fingers. A zip that went far enough for his fingertips to brush her buttocks and get lost in all the folds of her skirt. Not too lost, though, because he could cup his hand around a firm curve and pull her just close enough to leave her in no doubt about how much he wanted her.

Her tiny gasp beneath his lips and the way she pressed herself even closer was Dom's undoing.

It wasn't that those warnings weren't still there. If anything, in the last few minutes, the danger level had gone off the Richter scale because being with Emilia was everything he'd been afraid it would be and there would be no going back after this. Things were going to come crashing down around them and people might well be going to get hurt.

But that was going to happen anyway, wasn't it?

And he could handle the fallout. The hurt. But what about Emilia? The last thing Dom wanted to do was to hurt her. It might be the hardest thing he'd ever done but he could stop now, if that was what it took to protect her.

He held her face between his hands and waited for her eyes to focus.

'Do you want this, Emmy?' His voice was rough. Raw, even. 'Because if we should stop, it needs to be now…'

'No…' Her voice was no more than a whisper. Almost a whimper. 'Please…don't stop… I do want this…' He heard the way her breath hitched. 'Even if it is just for tonight…'

Just for tonight. He'd thought that tonight was his last chance, too. The last opportunity to cling to all the things he loved about the life he'd created away from his home and his royal heritage. Maybe it was the same for Emilia? That she wanted to cling to what they'd had between them that they'd never been brave—or perhaps foolish—enough to confirm?

He'd told himself that he had to make the most of this magic night and this…being able to be as physically close as it was possible to be to another human would make this night one that he was going to remember for the rest of his life. Emilia wanted it as much as he did so this was going to be his gift to the most amazing woman he was ever going to know.

A night that she would also remember for the rest of her life.

Sliding his hands up her back again, it took only a nudge from his thumbs on her shoulders to dislodge the lace straps that were still holding her dress up. The fabric rippled free and tumbled into a huge puddle on the marble tiles of this entranceway. The only underwear Emilia was wearing were a pair of lace panties the same colour as that dress and, as Dom dragged his gaze back to her eyes, he could see the hint of fear in them. *Dio mio…* did she think that he might not find her beautiful enough? Or change his mind about how much he wanted her?

He scooped her into his arms to carry her into his bedroom.

'You have no idea, do you, *mi amore*?' he murmured.

Her head was tucked in beneath his collar bone. Right against his heart. 'Of what?'

Dom kicked the bedroom door shut behind them. 'Of just how perfect you are…'

Oh… Dear Lord…

Emilia had never been so…what on earth was the word she needed? She was physically, emotionally, *sexually* exhausted and yet she'd never felt so alive. Or so happy.

So…so *whole*…

The way that Dom's breathing had slowed suggested that he had already fallen asleep and Emilia should follow his example because, while she had no idea of the time, dawn couldn't be that far away. She'd lost count of how many times they'd made love since Dom had carried her to his bed and the need for each other had been equally fierce on both sides. They both knew that their lives were going to go in such different directions very soon and it seemed that they'd made a tacit agreement to make the most of this one night because it could be the only one they ever got.

And it was a night that Emilia would never, ever forget.

With her eyes closed, tucked under Dom's arm, she rested her cheek against his chest where she could both feel and hear the steady beat of his heart. It was a big thing for her to be this close to someone else. When she'd told Dom about her past relationship with Chandler and said that she was happier on her own, anyway, she'd been quite sincere.

One of Emilia's earliest memories was a place where she'd discovered she could be completely alone and nobody could find her—a hole in the bottom of a hedge, just big enough for a little girl to crawl into and hide away from angry voices or frightening things. Being lonely was worth it to feel safe. At school, libraries became a haven away from bullies and her preferred exercise of running had always been a solitary activity. When she'd escaped that disastrous relationship with Chandler, there was such enormous relief to be found in being alone that Emilia had been able to ignore the loneliness that went with it. To close her eyes to the emptiness that her future threatened to include.

Yes…it had been well ingrained, that belief that she was happier on her own.

Until now…

Now, she knew what it was like to feel like *this*… As if she was hiding away in the safest place possible but she could never feel lonely again. She had someone with her who understood exactly who she was and why she was like that and he still wanted to be with her. Someone who thought she was…perfect?

Emilia lifted her head just enough to see Dom's face in the soft light of this room. *He* was the perfect one and she was missing him already. How crazy was that? He was right here but he had retreated into sleep. The black lashes that matched his, oh, so rumpled hair right now were resting on his cheeks. Deep, even breaths were coming through that gorgeously defined, Italian nose of his and his lips were ever so slightly parted and curled up at the corners, as if he was already dreaming of something very pleasant.

The temptation to touch those lips—kiss them again, perhaps—was strong but Emilia knew she wasn't going to risk waking him. She didn't want him to look at her and see what she was thinking. To know just how much she was going to miss him. Because, if he saw that, he would feel sorry for her because they both knew how unlikely it was that they would ever see each other again in the future. And Emilia didn't want to see that sympathy because that would be the end of this magical night and she wanted to feel like this for a little longer.

To feel safe. And loved. And whole…

Very gently, she let her head settle again in that spot where she could hear every beat of Dom's heart. A soft drum that was already pulling her into sleep but Emilia was fighting the pull. Because she didn't need to sleep—she was already dreaming…

It was the vibration from his ringing phone that woke Dom and he was startled to find his bedroom bathed in the first fingers of daylight through windows whose curtains had not been pulled. Sunrise at this time of year in Seattle didn't happen before about eight a.m. and he never normally slept this late. But then again, last night had been anything but normal, hadn't it? He could feel the weight of Emilia's head on his arm and it was obvious that she was still soundly asleep which was hardly surprising after he'd kept her awake for most of the night.

But…*oddio*…it had been a night he was definitely never, ever going to forget.

Carefully, Dom eased his arm from beneath her head and rolled away, picking up his phone as he got out of bed and moving swiftly towards the door of his en suite bathroom so as not to disturb Emilia just yet.

He had to take this call because he'd seen the name of caller on the screen.

'What is it, Max?'

'We've just completed the scan on your father,' Max Granger told him. 'I'm sorry Dom, but it's not good news…'

CHAPTER EIGHT

SPLASHING SO MUCH cold water on his face in the wake of that phone call should have been enough to bring Dom firmly back into the present but, as he knotted a towel around his waist for decency, he found himself standing beside his bed, pausing to take a deep, deep breath as his gaze rested on Emilia.

Taking a moment to forget everything that was rushing towards him and soak in the beauty of this woman. The flicker of fire that her hair made, tumbling against the crisp white of his bed linen. That pale, perfect skin that tasted as good as it looked and those freckles… He had a vague memory of vowing to kiss every single one of them…

Dom could almost feel himself being torn in two, here.

What half of him wanted, so much it felt like a shade of desperation, was to turn the clock back. Just a few hours. To when he'd scooped Emilia into his arms to carry her off to bed. This time, however, he'd close the curtains and turn his phone off and give them complete privacy for a little longer.

But time had run out.

The other half of himself was just as desperate to be near his father as Roberto faced a new crisis. And to talk to his sister, as he'd told Max he would do as soon as possible. It was a no-brainer where his duty lay and what his priorities were and Dom absolutely wanted to be there for his family immediately but he knew, too well, how hard it was going to be to walk away from Emilia.

Because he sensed that this would mark the beginning of the end.

If he had a choice, Dom would never want this to end. It had occurred to him during the gala last night that Emilia was someone that he could easily fall in love with if circumstances were very different. He'd taken the risk of playing with that fantasy, even, and giving himself a night of pretending that things *could* be that different only to find that it wasn't simply a possibility. He'd hidden it so well he hadn't even seen it himself but he was already in love with her and he proba-bly had been for far longer than he knew. Not that that was likely to change anything, of course. Reality was hovering, ready to crash all around him. Around them both...

As if she sensed that she was being watched, Emilia stirred in her sleep and stretched like a cat. Perhaps she was instinc-tively reaching out to touch him because Dom could see her muscles tense and pause as her arm swept the space that was probably still warm from his body. Her eyes flew open but it took a moment for her to register where she was and that he was standing beside the bed, and then to chase enough sleep from her eyes to really focus.

For a heartbeat, and then another, as he saw the dream filled haze lifting in her gaze, Dom couldn't help taking this fraction of time to snatch the last piece of that fan-tasy. To imagine an entirely different world, where he would see this transformation in her face every single morning for the rest of his life. That softening around her eyes that was reaching her lips now to become the be-ginnings of a smile, as if seeing *him* was the best thing that could possibly happen in those first moments of waking up to a new day. It looked…and felt…an awful lot like love. Was it possible that Emilia felt the same way about him as he was feeling about her? That, if she had her choice, she would want him to stay here? To stay with *her*?

He could fight for that. Somehow…

But, in just another heartbeat, Emilia's face changed again. The focus was far more intense and the embryonic smile vanished.

'What's wrong, Dom? What's happened?'

How could she read him so easily when he hadn't even been consciously thinking about what was worrying him so much?

'I just got a call from Max,' he told her. 'They've finished the scan on my father and he's not happy with what they've found. The tumour is growing and it's starting to cause problems. His intracranial pressure is rising.'

'Oh, no…' Emilia sat up, pulling the sheet to wrap around herself like a toga. 'They were hoping he'd recover more from the last surgery before they went ahead with removing the tumour, weren't they?'

Dom nodded. 'There's a few more tests to run and then a detailed plan has to be made for a challenging surgery like this. He's wanting to print a 3D anatomical model for a physical simulation of the surgery.'

'Wow...' Emilia looked fascinated. 'I've heard about that technology. I'll bet I could use it myself in some cases.'

It was so much easier to ease back into reality by slipping into a familiar, professional space. 'I'm sure you could. It'll certainly help Max and his team by letting them see exactly what the tumour looks like and how it sits in relation to blood vessels and surrounding brain structures.'

'How urgent is the surgery?'

'I guess that will depend on whether his condition remains stable or not but Max said something about the fifteenth—the day after tomorrow. Ironically, that's the date that his elective surgery was originally scheduled for.'

'I'll go and see him today,' Emilia said. 'I've been more than happy with the way his leg has been healing but I'd like to make sure the fixation is robust enough to cope with any movement that might be involved in the surgery.' She glanced towards the windows and blinked. 'What time *is* it?'

'Just before eight. What time are you due at work?'

'I've got a late start at eleven a.m. I thought it might be prudent after a big night out.'

She caught his gaze and, for a long moment, a silence hung between them. A silence that acknowledged everything that had happened in the last twelve, life-changing hours. Dom could feel that tearing sensation again, forcing the two halves of himself further apart.

'I'm due at nine a.m.,' he said. 'And I'll need to be a lot earlier if I can be so I can see my father and talk to my sister. I'm sorry... I'll have to jump into the shower and get going.' He cleared his throat, still holding that gaze. Clinging to it, in fact, with his words no more than a murmur. 'I'd rather be jumping back into bed...'

Emilia got to her feet. The look she was giving him was sharp enough to make him remember the countless times she had needled him into responding to a challenge or teased him because she'd already won.

'You're not a very good listener, are you? Or maybe you've just forgotten the pearls of wisdom I bestowed on you when we were discussing Thanksgiving that day?' She shook her head. 'I guess it was a long time ago. Nearly three weeks.' Her lips quirked and then she held his gaze and spoke slowly, enunciating every word separately as if she was speaking to someone of very limited intelligence. She even put her hand flat against his bare chest, near his heart, as if she wanted to emphasise just how important this was.

'Family. Is. Everything.'

There was a gleam in her eyes that softened any put down and her voice softened as well. 'Your family needs you and you need them, Dom. That has to come above absolutely everything else.'

Still he hesitated. Was he hoping that Emilia would arrange a time and space they could meet again later today? Or that she might offer to go with him?

Instead, her breath came out in a sigh. 'You still don't realise how lucky you are to have a family, Dom. It's something I always dreamed of having but I never have. I never will have…'

Dom shook his head. 'You could. You could make your own.'

Maybe it wouldn't be with him but he still wanted this astonishing woman to find the happiness she deserved in life.

But now it was Emilia who was shaking her head. 'I tried that, remember? With Chandler. Didn't work and I should have known it wouldn't. I can look after myself, Dom. Always have and always will be able to. And I'm happy on my own. It's better this way.'

The touch of her hand on his chest increased in pressure enough to become a shove to send him on his way. 'Go... Get clean. I'm going to find some of your gym gear or something to borrow so I don't have to do the taxi ride of shame in my ballgown.'

Was it possible that the memory of a single touch could be powerful enough to become a kind of scar?

Dom was beginning to think that it was possible, given that he was losing count of how many times he could still feel the imprint of Emilia's hand on his chest as he juggled the next, difficult forty-eight hours. There had been intense conversations with his sister and their father's neurosurgeon as results came in from examinations and tests and more scans. Time spent by his father's bedside were coloured by all the anxiety and guilt and even grief in knowing that these could be their last moments together and Dom had not been able to let his father know how much he was loved.

There were flashes of more guilt because he hadn't seen or spoken to Emilia since they'd spent that extraordinary night together but he knew she would understand that his family had to come first right now. She had, after all, reminded him of that in no uncertain terms.

He'd been successful in barely missing a beat in his beloved ER as well, because keeping himself as busy as possible and as distracted from any personal issues as possible was by far the best way he could deal with such enormous pressure. It meant that when he wasn't needed in the ER, he had to find other things that were challenging or interesting enough to take his entire focus and that was why he'd come up to one of Seattle General's operating theatres this morning. Not to check out where his own father was going to be, for probably many, many hours, later today but to follow up on a patient who'd captured his interest weeks ago.

Fourteen-year-old Jason, who had technically died when his heart had stopped beating almost as soon as he'd arrived by ambulance after his fainting episode at school, was due to have an implantable defibrillator inserted into his chest because extensive testing had shown that he had an inherited condition that had thickened the muscle of his heart enough to disrupt the way its electrical system worked. It was a procedure that Dom had never got around to watching so what better way to fill in some of the time before he was due to start his shift in the ER. He would still be able to visit his father before his surgery was scheduled to begin.

Dom pulled a hat and mask from the dispensers in the scrubbing in room adjacent to the theatre. He could see Jason already on the table in front of him and the anaesthetist was administering his sedation and watching vital signs, adjusting the volume of an alarm on one of the monitors. The beeping from the machine reminded Dom of that cardiac arrest alarm he'd heard that had signalled the moment he'd become involved in this case.

He'd been in his office. Talking to Emilia in the wake of her reaction to learning the truth about who he was. It wasn't just an echo of the alarm he could hear, however. He could hear some of his own words.

I guess I just don't want to lose what we have, Emmy. Something that's real. Something I can trust...

And...there it was again. The imprint of her hand burning the skin beneath the cotton of his scrub tunic. Disturbing enough to make him touch the spot himself to try and erase the sensation by rubbing at it.

The movement earned him a sharp sideways glance from the attending cardiologist who was reaching for a sterile towel to dry his hands.

'Chest pain, Dom?' He raised his eyebrows. 'You've come to the right place, then. Shall I see if we've got a spare defibrillator lying around that we could bung in?'

'I only came to watch, Rick.' But Dom felt like he was smiling for the first time in the last two days. Maybe because the physician's remark reminded him of the kind of banter he and Emilia had always shared? 'I like your bedside manner, though. It's true what they say about you, isn't it?'

Both men were grinning as they entered the theatre for what should be a routine and relatively minor procedure but one that had the potential to ensure that young Jason would go on to live a normal life that wasn't shadowed by the threat of sudden death.

Dom's smile faded as he stood back to watch the team's well-practised routine of implanting the cardioverter defibrillator. An incision was made under Jason's collarbone to form the pocket for the small device and wires were threaded through a large vein to be positioned in the heart's chambers under X-ray. Then it was time to test the device.

'These things are getting more sophisticated all the time,' Rick told him. 'You'll see, when we get him into VF.'

Dom glanced to where the electrophysiology technician was ready with his equipment.

'We synchronise a small shock to hit the T wave in the ECG,' the technician told him. 'It's the fastest and most effective way to induce ventricular fibrillation.'

'Don't worry…' Rick must have seen the look on Dom's face at the idea of deliberately causing a potentially fatal heart rhythm. 'We've got back up to deal with a cardiac arrest if the internal defib doesn't do its job.'

It took a few minutes to test the device that was capable of delivering a series of low-voltage electrical impulses to pace the heart, a small shock to try and correct the rhythm or a larger shock to deal with the heart stopping completely. Dom found himself holding his breath as he watched the screens of the monitors, waiting for that small device to do what it had taken a whole team in the ER to achieve that day that Jason had been his patient.

'And that's it,' Rick announced a short time later. 'We just need to close the incision and it'll be a wrap. We'll keep him in overnight, though, just to keep an eye on him.'

As Dom was leaving the suite of operating theatres, he passed an area where relatives were allowed to wait until they could visit the recovery room and be reassured that their loved one had made it through their surgery. He recognised Jason's mother, even though she was sitting with her head bowed, one hand on her forehead. He wanted to stop and reassure her but he'd misjudged the timing of the procedure a little and he was running late to be in the ER. He also knew that she wouldn't have to suffer much longer because Rick would be coming to see her within minutes to tell her how well the procedure had gone.

That pushing the elevator button would

trigger yet another memory of Emilia's touch on his chest was unexpected. Was it the pushing sensation or the fact that he'd just seen a mother who was desperately worried about her son which was an echo of more than Emilia's touch? He could hear *her* words this time.

'Family is everything...'

And, in turn, that brought a flood of memories of Thanksgiving Day. The laughter. The terrible cooking. The way Emilia had made him feel lucky to have a family, because even with their problems, it was so much more than she'd ever had in her life. Her relationship with that bastard, who couldn't recognise what he'd been lucky enough to have and had undermined her ability to achieve everything she was capable of achieving, had been an attempt to create a family of her own, hadn't it? And its failure had been damaging enough to make her believe she was better off—and would be happier—on her own?

Oh...*sì*... Dom could feel that push on his chest with vivid clarity.

The sensation of being pushed out of Emilia's life.

She didn't feel the same way about him as he did about her. She wasn't remotely interested in forming another permanent relationship and even if she was, she wouldn't want any part of the future that now lay before him.

Abruptly, Dom turned away from the elevator that still hadn't arrived. He gave the firestop door at the entrance to the staircase a firm shove and then took the steps at a fast pace. He needed to be somewhere else. Somewhere he'd be too busy to keep thinking about Emilia like this.

Of course she wouldn't want a part of his future. She loved her work here as much as he did. And she'd always been a private person when it came to her personal life. Dom could be quite sure he wasn't the only person who'd known her for so many years but had no clue what her early life had been like. Imagine if she was put under the scrutiny of the media who would stop at nothing to reveal information that would sell their publications? What could be better than a princess with a past that was far juicier than simply being a commoner?

He wouldn't want that for Emilia. And he knew that it would be the last thing she would want for herself. She'd learned to hide that part of her life. She'd said herself that she'd learned to look after herself and succeed against the odds and Dom could be sure that she would continue to do that. And that she'd thrive.

Dom was almost at the ER now and he would be able to immerse himself in what would hopefully be a very busy shift. He had cover, as well, so he could take breaks to be with Giada as she waited for their father to come out of surgery—probably in the same room that Jason's mother had been waiting.

Emilia was quite right. Family *was* everything and he had to look after his, especially today. Memories of his night with Emilia and any dreams of her being a part of his life in the future had to be dismissed. He'd managed before, when he'd totally dismissed his attraction to Emilia when he'd first seen her at medical school. He could do it again now.

Because the persona of Dr. Domenico di Rossi was getting ready to leave the building. His Royal Highness Domenico Baresi was about to step into those shoes and begin a totally different life.

He, too, needed to learn to look after himself. And thrive. Because he owed that, not only to his family, but to his country as well.

Emilia would understand because she understood *him*, probably better than anyone else ever had. Or ever would.

Trauma Team to ER. Stat.

The clock felt like it was being rewound as Emilia responded to her pager. Back to the day before any of this had started. Before she'd known Dom's secret and before she'd revealed so much about her own background. Before she'd fallen in love with someone she'd only ever seen as a rival and a colleague and so far before they'd become close enough to *make* love it felt like a different century.

The case was not that dissimilar to the one that had brought Dom's father and sister into the emergency room of Seattle General. A car had gone out of control, presumably because the flurries of snow happening today had made the surface slippery, and the driver had been powerless to stop the vehicle hitting a pedestrian at high speed.

The scene in Resus One was almost identical. Dom was there, gathering his team around him as they all donned their protective gear of gowns, gloves and goggles. He was

supervising drugs being drawn up and ensur-
ing that specialised trolleys were available,
including the equipment for a FAST scan to
look for internal bleeding following abdominal or chest trauma. Dom being here was unexpected given that Emilia knew today was
the day his father was facing the challenge
of the surgery to remove his brain tumour.
She'd been to see the King more than once
in the last two days to confirm that she was
happy with the stability of his healing femoral fracture but this was the first time she'd
seen Dom since she'd left his apartment on
the morning after the gala ball.

The usual heightened senses of the adrenaline rush of a trauma team code made Emilia's response to seeing Dom so acute it felt
more physical than emotional. And there were
far deeper layers than mere surprise. There
was delight to be found but apprehension as
well. And hope…? She'd been fine with not
having heard anything from him in the last
forty-eight hours because she'd told herself
that he had too much going on with his family and she hadn't wanted to intrude by con-
tacting him for the same reason.

She knew she was staring as she stepped

into the resuscitation area and she knew that Dom was aware that she was here. The moment of truth came in the split second before Emilia turned to reach for a pair of gloves from the wall dispenser and Dom looked up and directly at her. Again, it was only for a blink of time but it was long enough for Emilia to feel a shiver run down her spine. The clock really had rewound and her apprehension had not been misplaced. This was purely professional. She had reverted to being nothing more than a colleague. A rival. Whatever barriers had been there before any of this had started were back in place and the connection that had been so powerful such a short time ago was nowhere to be seen or felt.

And it *hurt*, dammit…

It was far more than a slap in the face. It was devastating. Even though Emilia had known that there was never going to be anything more than that one night together, she would have expected there to be an acknowledgment that that private connection would always be there. That it was now rather more significant than it ever had been, in fact.

It would be totally unprofessional to let a personal emotional issue distract her right

before the arrival of a probably critically injured patient. It was not something that had
ever threatened Emilia's focus before and she
wasn't about to let it happen now. Maybe she
was actually wrong and Dom was only as focussed as he ever was when he was leading
the trauma team with the added tension of
his family worries in the background. They'd
always had their own way of dealing with
tension and old habits often became an automatic response.

'You've been busy,' Emilia said lightly. 'I
love what you've done to the place.'

He was frowning at her in bemusement.
Emilia tilted her head towards the fat string of
red tinsel that was wound around an IV pole
and the bunches of fake holly that adorned
the twelve-lead ECG trolley.

Dom's frown became a scowl as he turned
to snap at a nurse. 'Who did this? It's totally
inappropriate to have Christmas decorations
in an area where we bring critically ill patients. Get rid of them. Stat.'

With her arms full of tinsel and holly, the
nurse crossed paths with the stretcher that
was rushed in moments later so Emilia had
no time to dwell on a side of Dom she'd never

seen before and wonder just how much stress he was under to have reacted like that. Worse, to feel that, despite feeling so hurt herself, she wanted to help him. Just to touch his arm, perhaps, and catch his gaze for long enough to somehow let him know that she was here if he needed her. That she understood…

Perhaps it was just as well that the familiar chaos of an incoming patient required the absolute attention of every member of the medical team ready to treat them. And this patient, Simon, a thirty-five-year-old man most definitely needed a lot of help if he was going to survive. Paramedics had applied a pelvic binder because they suspected Simon had a fractured pelvis and everyone here knew that the force needed to cause a significant injury to this solid bony structure made it very likely that he would have other significant injuries. Like chest trauma. Broken bones. A ruptured spleen could explain why Simon's blood pressure was dropping to an alarming level if there were no major vessels damaged as a result of the blunt force of a car hitting his pelvis.

Everybody was flat out from the moment Simon was brought in.

'Let's get another large bore IV in, stat, please.' Dom was watching the readings on the monitors coming into focus. 'And get some fluids up. Simon, can you hear me? Do you know where you are?'

The response was no more than an agonised groan.

'We need some more analgesia on board. Have we got some fentanyl drawn up yet? Ketamine?'

Technicians, interns and nurses were working around each other in a familiar, well-rehearsed dance as soon as Simon had been transferred from the ambulance gurney. Clothing was being removed. Blood taken. Electrodes attached for monitoring.

'I want a chest X-ray,' Dom ordered. 'A FAST scan. Pelvic X-ray.' His instructions were crisp and clear. 'What's the blood pressure now?'

'Systolic ninety.'

'Type and cross match. We're going to need some blood. Don't rock the pelvis. And no log roll, please. We don't want any unnecessary movement.'

It was Dom who placed his gloved hands

gently under Simon's back to palpate for any major wounds or bone deformity.

'It's clear,' he said, standing back as the overhead X-ray machines were rolled in to take images. 'Okay…anyone without a lead apron step outside, please.'

Emilia had been close enough to examine Simon's chest and found some probably broken lower ribs which could well have lacerated his spleen or liver but she was holding her breath to see what the X-rays would reveal was going on much lower in his abdomen. Despite the aggressive fluid resuscitation this young man was receiving, his blood pressure indicated that he was in hypovolaemic shock which could rapidly prove fatal if they couldn't find and stop whatever internal bleeding was going on.

'Look. There and there…' Dom had come to look over Emilia's shoulder as soon as she had the image up on the computer screen. 'Nasty pelvic ring fracture. Clearly unstable with that anteroposterior displacement of at least a centimetre. Maybe one point five.'

'We need to get him to Theatre for a laparotomy. There might not be enough blood to be showing up on the FAST scan but I'd put money on his spleen being ruptured thanks to those rib fractures. I'm going to aspirate next but his BP's already so low it's not safe to wait for a CT scan.'

'He needs external fixation to stabilise his pelvis before anyone goes near his spleen. The pelvic binder has to come off to allow access and if you open up the abdomen and start shifting organs around without fixation, it could disrupt the pelvic fractures and he could lose his entire blood volume into the pelvic cavity before anyone gets near his spleen.'

'You want to do that here?'

'Can do, if he's haemodynamically stable enough. It'll take me ten to fifteen minutes once we're set up and I can do it without X-ray.'

Emilia could actually feel Dom's focus. Could feel the way they were welded together as a team with a single focus and the absolute determination that they were going to win this battle. It didn't occur to her until later that this might well be the last time they could work together like this but it wouldn't have made any difference at the time, anyway. They always worked together like this.

Dom scrubbed in to help her. Simon was unconscious and oblivious to the preparations around him as staff numbers were reduced to a minimum, his body was draped and the skin of his lower abdomen prepped for the surgical procedure. The sterile packs had been rolled open on the top of a trolley, with an impressive array of steel pins and bars and a drill along with scalpels and sutures but it was a felt pen marker that Emilia reached for first.

'I'm marking the anterior superior iliac spine with an X,' she told Dom. 'And the inferior with a circle. I'll do that on both sides before I make my first incision.'

It took fifteen minutes to construct a frame that would make it possible to move Simon and perform the open surgery he was going to need without exacerbating an injury that could easily prove fatal. It was a challenging fifteen minutes that had trickles of sweat dampening the back of Emilia's tunic and she blew out a relieved breath as she tightened the last bolt.

'You can let go now, thanks, Dom. We should be completely stable now.' Grasping the top of the triangular frame, she tipped it carefully a little to one side. The whole of Simon's pelvis moved as one piece. This frame would not only keep his bones in position until they healed, it meant it was safe to shift him to Theatre and tackle any other sources of blood loss.

'Let's get him up to Theatre,' Dom instructed, stepping back. But then he turned, with a smile and spoke quietly. 'Good job. Thanks, Emmy.'

The glow of that praise stayed with Emilia as she followed her patient to the theatre suite. Or maybe it was because the adrenaline rush of this case still had her senses heightened and she wasn't walking alone. Dom was staying with Simon until he could be handed over to the general surgeon who was waiting in an operating theatre for their arrival.

It wasn't as though it meant anything, though. Dom had always acknowledged the skills of anyone he worked with and a dramatic case like this was exactly what they both loved so much about their work. This was no more than the old dynamic between them but Emilia had new insight about why it had worked so well. They'd always competed so fiercely and baited each other so

mercilessly because that kind of a relationship could actually be passionate but still
completely safe. Had they both instinctively
known how painful it would be to take those
protective barriers away only to have to re-
build them?

There was a new team to take over the
management of the next stage of Simon's
treatment but Emilia was going to stay in
Theatre. It was quite possible that this pelvic injury would need internal fixation and,
while she would normally want to wait a few
days for bleeding and swelling to be under
control, if the patient was having abdominal
surgery for other reasons, it might be preferable to take the opportunity for any further
orthopaedic work.

'I might stay for a while, too,' Dom said.
'I've got cover in the ER anyway, because I
knew I'd have to leave at some point today.'

'Is your…? I mean, has the surgery started?'

A single nod. 'It's been going for some time
already. I get progress reports and pass them
on to Giada. They'll tell me when it's over
but, until then, I really need to keep busy.'

Emilia's lips curved gently in sympathy. 'It
helps, doesn't it?'

Another nod. A flash of something in his eyes that told her he *was* still feeling their connection but it was drowned instantly by something that looked a lot like sadness.

'I don't need to scrub in so I'll leave you to get on with it.'

He turned away but Emilia paused before entering the theatre's anteroom. She wanted to call softly to Dom. To make him turn around again so that she could get another glimpse of what she knew was still there.

She wanted to whisper something.

I love you...

I miss you already...

But what did she expect to happen? That he would reject what his family—his whole country probably—wanted? Or that she would decide she could walk away from what had been the total focus of her life for as long as she wanted to remember? Her dedication to her career had already destroyed a relationship. She'd spent too long putting herself and her ambitions above everything else. Prince Domenico Baresi deserved far more than that in a partner.

She might be doing them both a favour by letting him go.

Figuratively and literally. At least for now, when he was clearly struggling to cope with everything life was throwing at him. It wasn't as if she had a choice, anyway, because a nurse was coming along the corridor towards Dom.

'Dr di Rossi? I was just coming down to the ER to find you. Your patient that you asked to be informed about—Mr Baresi? He's out of Theatre and has been taken through to Recovery.'

Dom walked away from Emilia without a backward glance.

And she turned to walk away as well. Into Theatre. A place that felt like a sanctuary right now. Like home. But then, this was the place where she really belonged, after all.

Perhaps it was destined to be the only place that would ever feel like home.

CHAPTER NINE

OKAY. IT WAS OFFICIAL.

Emilia hated Christmas.

For some reason that ability she had honed during her life to ignore or tolerate all the hype of the season had deserted her this year in the final run up to the big day.

There was a palpable pressure to keep such negativity private but Emilia knew she wasn't alone in feeling like a Grinch. There were so many people out there for whom the inescapable message that this was the time for families to come together and show their love for each other by bestowing gifts and sharing a fabulous feast would rub salt into wounds that could never properly heal. People who had lost a loved one at this time of year, perhaps. At worst, a child or baby, which would make this all the more agonising with small faces radiating excitement as they counted down the sleeps. There were the people who were estranged from their families for whatever reasons. And then there were those who simply didn't have a family.

People like Emilia.

So, yeah… Christmas was something to be endured, not enjoyed for her and it seemed to be getting more intense with every passing day. It was going to be Christmas Eve tomorrow so it had to be peaking any moment now but it couldn't come soon enough for Emilia and she was beginning to rethink her usual strategy of trying to bury herself in her work. Maybe next year she would take a month off to go to a place that didn't celebrate Christmas. Like Vietnam, perhaps. Or Qatar. Or Outer Mongolia? That way she wouldn't be faced with constant reminders of what she would prefer to ignore. The resuscitation areas in the ER and the operating theatres might be mercifully free of decorations or music or flashing lights but the rest of Seattle General had become more and more festive as the countdown to Christmas ramped up.

Gifts were piling up under the huge trees in the atrium, ready to be distributed to in-patients in the children's wards. Every second person was wearing something festive like the snowman earrings a young woman at the main reception desk had on today. Yesterday, Emilia had even seen an orderly dressed in an adult-sized elf suit, for heaven's sake. There was tinsel everywhere, like the green, ECG rhythm strip that someone had cleverly stuck along the wall of the corridor she turned into. Her own patients who were admitted to the fracture clinic to have broken bones set or progress monitored and casts applied or changed were leaving with tartan bows or sprigs of plastic mistletoe attached to their casts and the only choice of colours at present were, of course, red or green.

Children were apparently embracing the season by wearing any favourite dress-up outfits. Like the small girl Emilia could see coming towards her now, dressed in a rather spectacular pink princess outfit, complete with a miniature crown and glittery shoes.

A *princess* costume?

Was this a cruel twist of fate, designed to mock the brief fantasy she had indulged in on the night of the gala, that she and Dom could be together for ever? That she could actually become a real princess?

It was almost the last straw. Emilia ducked into a staff toilet and turned on the cold water at the first basin. As she cupped her hands to catch some water, she caught sight of herself in the mirror and she was shocked to see her inner turmoil reflected so clearly in the tight lines of her face and the stormy blue of her eyes. The hurt was still there but there was something darker now, as well. Anger...

She hadn't seen or heard from Dom in a week now. Not since they'd worked together in the initial management of Simon's fractured pelvis—the patient she was on her way to see at the moment, in fact. And, okay, she knew he had a hell of a lot going on in his own life right now but she didn't deserve to be treated like this. Pushing her out of his life was his prerogative and had, no doubt, been inevitable in the long run but surely he could see that, for her, this would be tapping into a lot of old stuff that had had such a negative impact on her life and still had the ability to do her head in. Being pushed out of families. Changing schools. Feeling unwanted and unloved. Dreaming that life could magically become perfect with a fresh start until the dream had been shattered too many times to bother dusting it off.

The splash of cold water helped disperse the fragments of unpleasant emotions. Hurt. Anger. Sadness. By the time Emilia reached for some paper towels to pat her face dry she could see the difference in her reflection. Nobody would guess that she had any kind of struggle going on. She was the calm, skilled, professional doctor she had fought so hard to become. Which meant that at least one of her dreams had come true. Clearly the most important one, given that it was a dream she could still believe in and one that would last for the rest of her life.

The smile that appeared slowly on the face of her patient when she entered Simon's room to check on him was enough to brighten what was left of Emilia's day.

'You look like you're feeling a whole lot better, Simon.'

He nodded. 'I even got out of bed this morning for long enough to use the chair instead of a bedpan.'

'How was that?' Emilia picked up the patient file clipped to the end of Jason's bed in the post-surgical orthopaedic ward.

'A bit rough,' Simon admitted.

'Did you use your pump to give yourself some more pain medication?'

'Yeah…'

'I know it's not easy.' After a quick scan of the notes and vital signs being recorded on the file, Emilia put it down and perched one hip on the end of Simon's bed. 'Especially at this stage of your healing, given that you've got quite a bit of hardware with those plates and screws that are holding your pelvis together, but it is very important that you are moving. Lying still for too long can lead to complications and we don't want you getting pneumonia or something.'

'I just want to get home, Doc. It's not going to be in time for Christmas, though, is it?'

'Afraid not,' she agreed. 'We can't let you go home until you can transfer yourself independently and have wheelchair mobility or are able to use crutches without weight bearing. That might take a couple of weeks but your physical therapist will be able to monitor your progress and make that call.'

'Is it true what the nurse told me today?

That I'm lucky to be alive and that what you did in the ER for me would have saved my life? He said if someone had moved me the wrong way, I could have bled to death in no time at all.'

'You were certainly in a bad way.' Emilia nodded. 'But it wasn't just me. There was a whole team of us looking after you that day.'

Including Dom… She wouldn't have been able to do her own job as well as she had if it hadn't been for the way the two of them could work as a team. Aside from anything more personal, she was going to miss having him leading Seattle General's ER trauma team.

'Can't believe it's been a week.' Simon lay back against his pillows and closed his eyes. 'I can only remember bits of it, so it feels like it's only been a couple of days.'

'Mmm…' Emilia found a smile. She had had the opposite impression in that this last week had felt far, far longer. 'Keep up the good work, Simon, and hopefully the rest of your stay with us will feel like it's gone just as quickly.'

The route Emilia took having left the ward took her close to the ER and the pull became too strong. But it would only be professional courtesy to let Dom know about the progress of a case that had come through his resuscitation area, wouldn't it? Especially when he always took an interest in following patients up.

His office was empty.

'He's not here,' a nurse told her, walking past to get to the staffroom.

'Do you know when he'll be back?'

'No idea. He's taken some leave. I did hear a rumour that he had some family visiting? Or a close friend of the family in hospital, perhaps? He might not be back until after Christmas if that's true. Did you need him for something urgent?'

'No.' Emilia shook her head. She didn't need Dom for anything urgent. What she needed him for was more like something impossible.

It made sense that Dom would have taken leave to be by his father's bedside and to support his sister. She knew that Roberto was being cared for in the most private area that this large hospital could provide and Dom would be being careful to keep his business equally private—especially if things weren't going so well in the aftermath of his father's brain surgery?

There was no reason for Emilia to stay here but, for a long moment, she stood in the doorway, thinking back to when she'd come into this office that day without knocking first, to see Dom with his head in his hands, looking shockingly broken. That had been the start of finding out just how little she knew about him, as a man rather than simply a rival. The start of new feelings that had, almost from the beginning, included huge empathy for what his future would hold, for the breakdown of his relationship with a father he clearly loved very much and also for how hard it was going to be for him to give up his beloved career.

Where had that empathy gone? It was pretty selfish to be indulging in feeling so hurt and angry given that such major areas of her own life weren't hanging in the balance. She wasn't in danger of losing a parent, having to protect a sibling or contemplating the responsibility of ruling a country. Dom was probably exhausted, she thought, both emotionally and physically. He probably didn't have anything left that would allow him to face any complication that she might be representing in his life. The best thing Emilia could do for both of them was to get out of the way but knowing that Dom might be hurting and not being able to offer any comfort was enough to bring the prickle of tears that were never going to fall.

This was by no means the first time in her life that Emilia had needed to pull herself together and to sort out a messed-up head and bruised heart and, as she prepared to make her way home on this freezing winter evening, she realised that she already knew the best first step to deal with all of this. Mind you, it could be a bit more difficult to tap into that resource at this time of year, especially after the snowfalls of the last few days.

Emilia went online in her office to check the weather forecast for tomorrow and, while it would be cold enough for any snow lying around to be in no danger of melting, the forecast was for clear skies and to be calm enough to not present too much of an obstacle with the windchill factor. She clicked onto other websites after that, checking both road conditions around Seattle and the timetable for the ferries that crossed Puget Sound to Bainbridge Island or Southport.

A few minutes later, Emilia sat back in her chair, closed her eyes and breathed out a long sigh of relief.

She still had a spot of shopping to do on her way home but she now had a plan in place to get to the one space that was almost guaranteed to offer her the peace of mind she so desperately needed.

She could do this.

He couldn't do this any longer.

Not for today. He should have gone home long ago for a shower and some sleep but Dom had lingered by his father's bedside this evening. Something was different and his instincts as a physician were keeping him here. Watching every monitor. And yes…there were more blips than usual in the tracing of his father's heart rate and rhythm. Missed beats and an acceleration here and there in the rates of both heart and breathing. His father's temperature had risen a fraction too.

Was this the beginning of the end? A sign of an infection? Or was Roberto in so much pain he was aware of it even though he was still unconscious? Whatever it was, Dom wasn't about to leave until he figured it out. Even as one hour bled into another as the first hours of Christmas Eve approached. He was exhausted to the point of barely functioning so, when he saw it, he thought it was simply wishful thinking. A figment of his imagination.

Until he saw it again.

Along with another, unsettling, disruption of the cardiac monitor, he saw a twitch of his father's fingers as they curled and then relaxed again. Dom was holding his breath as he raised his head to look at his father's face where he could see the flutter of his eyelids as they opened. For the longest moment, Roberto stared at his son without any sign of recognition and then his eyes drifted shut again.

Oddio... Dom closed his eyes, dipping his head against the sudden wave of pain that was threatening to overwhelm him. Was this the worst thing that could happen? That his father would regain consciousness but be so brain-damaged he wouldn't even recognise his own son?

He called Max, who arrived in the private room with commendable swiftness and he stayed as Max performed a thorough neurological examination. Roberto might look as if he was still in a coma but he was responsive to painful stimuli and even talking to him could create subtle differences in his vital signs like heart rate and blood pressure.

'He's waking up,' Max agreed when they discussed the results. 'He's slipped back into unconsciousness now but it's still very good news. His LOC is a lot lighter and he could wake up more definitively at any time. I'll stay in the hospital and come and look in every couple of hours. Unless you'd like me to stay?

Dom shook his head. 'I'd like to be the first person he sees when he wakes up.'

'Of course.' Max shook his hand. 'Just page me if you're worried about anything.'

Dom dozed on and off in the comfortable armchair beside the bed for an hour. And then another. He was getting a minimal amount of rest but it wasn't real sleep—he was still aware and alert for any changes in the soft beeping from the monitors around the bed. And the sound of his father taking an uneven breath and letting it out in a sigh.

'… Dom? You're here…?'

Dom's eyes flew open as he jerked his head up to find that Roberto's eyes were also open. This time, he could see the recognition in them and relief flooded his heart so much it felt like it might burst.

'Papa? Are you in pain? I'll call Max…'

'No… Don't go, Dom…'

'But I must contact Giada. She's been so worried. We've…' Dom had to clear his throat. 'We've been waiting a while for you to wake up, you know?'

'What day is it, son?'

'Christmas Eve. Very early. It's…' Dom checked his watch. 'Coming up to four a.m. now.'

Roberto blinked slowly, his head sinking back into his pillow. 'Don't disturb her, then,' he said softly. 'Not yet. Don't disturb anyone. It's you I need to talk to, Domenico. It's why I came here. I… I've been asleep too long, haven't I?' He was frowning now as he looked up at Dom. 'What happened?'

'There was a car accident the day you arrived. You broke your leg and had a head injury.'

Roberto reached out to grip Dom's hand. 'Giada? Was she hurt?'

'No. She's fine. She went back home to look after things. She's been back to see you, of course, but she's in Isola Verde again now. She's been very worried and we've been talking every day…but…you're going to be fine, Papa. The surgery to remove your tumour went perfectly. We were just waiting for you to wake up…' Dom's voice trailed into silence and he had to blink back the tears that were filling his eyes.

Neither man said anything for a minute. And then another. Dom scanned every monitor but couldn't see anything that was alarming so there was no need to call Max in. Roberto still needed to rest but Dom wasn't going anywhere because this time, with just a father and son, was undeniably precious. He'd be here when Roberto woke up again. And… even if his father was falling asleep again now, this was an opportunity he couldn't miss.

'I love you, Papa… I'm sorry I've never told you that before…'

Roberto's eyes opened slowly—eyes that were exactly the same dark shade as Dom's— and he held Dom's gaze.

'That's not your fault,' he told his son. 'It

was mine. I never said it to you, did I? I was too hard on you. You and your sister. We lost your mother too early, I think, and… I didn't handle it well. I'm sorry, Dom. That was why I came here early. To talk to you about…' He closed his eyes again, as if too fatigued.

'I know,' Dom murmured. 'You came to tell me that it's time I did my duty. I should have stepped up long ago and let you have the abdication you deserve. I'm ready…'

But Roberto rolled his head slowly, from one side to the other, making a negative gesture even though it was clearly painful for him.

'No… I came to tell you that, of course, I want you to succeed me but I will respect whatever choice you make. That I will still love you…'

Dom swallowed hard. He had a choice? Was his father offering him the chance to stay here and keep his career? To be with *Emilia*?

'I've been dreaming,' Roberto told him. 'So much. Of you. I understand now why your career is so important to you. Why it's so much of who you are… I respect that passion, my son. And your gift…'

A weight was falling off Dom's shoulders.

He didn't think his father had been dreaming, however. At some level, had he been listening to and absorbing all those late-night conversations as he lay in that coma for week after week? Did he understand things that Dom had never thought he could even explain well enough?

It was enough to feel that the distance between them had evaporated. That there was a bond here like no other and it was one that Dom couldn't turn his back on again, no matter what he was leaving behind.

'I understand things now, too.' He took his father's hand in his own and then put his other hand over the top of it as well. 'Someone… someone very special to me…has reminded me how lucky I am to have my family. To have a place that I belong and a chance to put things right. And yes… I've been able to do what I wanted to do so much. To *be* who I wanted to be for a long time. Longer than I deserved, perhaps. But I meant what I said, Papa. I'm ready to come home. I'm ready to accept my destiny. To rule Isola Verde and make you proud.'

'I've always been proud of you, Domenico. And we have a wonderful new hospital too, you know. They would be so proud to have their King as their patron.'

This time, as Roberto closed his eyes, Dom knew it was time to let him rest properly. A normal sleep, thank goodness, and not a pathological unconsciousness. He needed to call Giada and to let Max know that his father was awake and alert and there didn't seem to be any obvious deterioration in his mental faculties. He didn't want to disturb his father by making the calls in here, however.

'I'm going to go and let you sleep for a while, Papa.' Dom pushed himself to his feet, stiff and sore after sitting for so long. 'Max will be here soon to check on you again. It won't be long before it's a new day and there's going to be a lot of people who will be so happy to know that you're awake and on the road to a real recovery.'

Roberto gave a very slow nod, this time, but he didn't open his eyes when he spoke.

'This special person you talk of,' he murmured. 'Will she come home with you and be your Queen?'

'I…don't think that's possible. She's happy here. She's like me, Papa. She cares about her work more than anything else.'

'Are you sure?' There was a frown line between the King's eyes. 'You have to be sure, Dom. It's hard to do it alone. Believe me… I know…'

Was he sure?

Dom was sitting at the desk in his office some time later, his head in his hands as he fought off a weariness that was going to overwhelm him anytime now. There was no point in going home because he had made arrangements for an encrypted phone call that could maintain complete secrecy to happen between the hospital and the palace in Isola Verde which was timed for seven a.m., Seattle time. He'd already texted Giada to give her the wonderful news about their father but they couldn't go public yet. Palace officials would be gathering for the conference call because there were many decisions and plans to be made as they prepared statements about what was happening with the royal family in order to make an announcement about the succession of the throne of Isola Verde.

Rubbing at eyes that felt full of grit, Dom remembered that he'd sat like this, in this office, once before, hadn't he? When he'd been grappling with a similar sense of being overwhelmed. When Emilia had come in and he'd known that she'd seen past the protective shield he'd always had in place—especially with regard to her.

With a heartfelt sigh, Dom put his arms on his desk and lowered his head to rest his forehead on the cushion they provided. He'd learned to catnap as an intern and knew how valuable even a few minutes' sleep could be when he had to keep functioning for a double shift. It would only take seconds to fall into a state where his body—and mind—could gather enough new strength to keep him going.

Those few seconds were enough, however.

Enough for Dom to realise that his father had spoken wise words. It would be so hard to cope with his new future alone and he didn't want to. And...in spite of everything Emilia had told him, he wasn't at all sure that she really believed that she was happier facing life alone. She was too good at putting on a brave face, wasn't she? Of hiding how she really felt?

Maybe he was wrong and the career and home Emilia had struggled to win was more important than anything else in her life but the very least she deserved was to know that someone understood and respected that. That she had choices, if she wanted them.

And that she was loved *this* much…

CHAPTER TEN

A LITTLE SLEEP and a lot of strong coffee and handling the conference call to the palace was no problem. Dom felt even more awake as the group conversation ended, knowing that there was now a team of experts at work drafting the statements and press releases.

His private chat to Giada after the palace business had lifted his spirits even further. She would be on a plane as soon as she could tomorrow so that she would be able to see her father on Christmas Day. It would, in fact, be the first time in many years that the three of them would be together as a family for Christmas and that was going to be something to celebrate.

But he couldn't relax completely yet even if he was still on leave. There was something even more important to do and it was nearly eight a.m. Emilia could very well be at work already and Dom had to talk to her. He drained the mug of coffee on his desk, ran his fingers through his hair to try and comb it roughly, rubbed at his chin and decided not to worry about the stubble he had accumulated since yesterday, and got to his feet to open his office door.

Not that he could step out. Ayanna was standing in front of him. She had a laptop computer in her arms and…she didn't look happy.

'I'm so sorry, Dr di Rossi,' she said. 'But there's something you've got to see.'

It was unwanted publicity about Max. Someone had recognised the world-famous neurosurgeon and started asking questions about why he was here at Seattle General and why was there so much secrecy surrounding his extended visit. There were photographs of him leaving the hospital, of him and Ayanna leaving the gala ball and one of his wife who'd died a couple of years ago, with her famous husband having been unable to save her from the brain aneurysm she had suffered. It was horrible publicity for Max and Dom winced at seeing such private information being spread.

'This is my fault,' Ayanna said miserably. 'I was so focussed on keeping your family's information private that it never occurred to me that the press would go after Max.'

'It's unfortunate,' Dom agreed. 'And I'm very sorry Max has to go through this but it could have been a lot worse.' He smiled at Ayanna. 'You did one part of your job extremely well. We're going public with an announcement but it's going to take some time to get everything in place. Giada won't be back until tomorrow evening probably and we want the family to be together when the announcement is made so it's planned for the morning of the twenty-sixth.'

Ayanna nodded. 'I'll be ready. Do you want a press conference set up?'

'Yes. Thank you.' Dom glanced at his watch. 'I should go and check on my father and I expect Max won't be far away. Have you heard the great news that my father's awake now? That everything's looking very good?'

Ayanna nodded again. 'I'm so happy for you. I was so worried that he hadn't woken up yet.'

'Come with me,' Dom invited. 'And see for yourself. I'll introduce you, because my father will want some input into how the press conference is going to be handled.'

It would have to be a very brief introduction, however, because Dom was increasingly impatient to go and find Emilia before she got caught up, for hours perhaps, in an operating theatre.

He didn't even stop to sympathise with Max about the intrusion into his private life, when he came out of Roberto's room with Ayanna a short time later. He just shook the neurosurgeon's hand warmly.

'Thank you, Max, for everything you've done for my father. My family is in your debt for ever. Now, if you'll excuse me, I have something urgent to do...'

So urgent, he had to stop himself running down the last corridor that led to the orthopaedic department. The receptionist said she hadn't seen Dr Featherstone so far this morning but he could try the fracture room—a space that was already busy with the medical staff dealing with people who needed a new cast or urgent adjustments done in time for Christmas Day.

'Emilia's not here,' her senior resident told

Dom. 'She's been working about ten days straight but even then we had to force her to take a day off. She only agreed because she's rostered on for Christmas Day tomorrow. Ah…here we are.' He opened a drawer and picked up what looked like a bag of plastic leaves and berries. 'We thought we'd run out of bits of mistletoe to stick on the casts today.'

'Ah…okay…' Dom knew about mistletoe but couldn't see the point of putting it on a plaster cast. Weren't you supposed to stand beneath it to kiss someone? Anyway, he was already planning his next step which involved charming Emilia's secretary into providing the address of her boss's apartment. He didn't want to send a text message. What he wanted to say had to be done face to face. 'Thanks, anyway.'

'Hey…' the younger doctor was grinning. 'Take one of these.' He put a sprig of the plastic leaves into Dom's hand. 'You never know when you might need one. Merry Christmas…'

Dom didn't want to be rude so he smiled and shoved the plastic token into the back pocket of the jeans he was wearing. Emilia's office was nearby and her secretary was quite happy to provide her address to a close colleague on the trauma team. A short time after that, Dom was moving fast towards the nearest exit of Seattle General. It might still be early in the day but it felt like time was starting to run out.

Emilia's apartment block was within walking distance of the hospital. The sidewalks were damp and there was slushy snow filling the gutters but the sky was crisp and clear above. Dom filled his lungs with the cold air and kept his hands in the pockets of his jacket, walking as fast as he could past other pedestrians and across busy roads. He didn't need to waste time trying to find Emilia's name and doorbell on the bank of letterboxes in the entrance to her apartment block, because there was an elderly concierge in a small office right beside the automatic doors.

'Could you tell me which box belongs to Dr Featherstone, please?' he asked.

'Third one down in the second row,' the concierge told him helpfully.

Dom pressed the button, leaning closer to the small grill beside the button that would allow Emilia to ask who it was.

'She won't answer that,' the concierge said.

'Oh?' Dom turned back. 'Why not?'

'She headed out real early this morning.'

'Oh…' It was more than disappointment that Dom could feel wash over him. There was anxiety there, as well. And a sinking feeling that he really might be too late. 'Um… she didn't say when she'd be back, did she?'

'Nah…' The elderly man scratched at his chin. 'But she was carrying a whole load of stuff. Like she was going camping or some such.' He shook his head. 'She even had a pair of snow shoes, would you believe? I didn't know what they were so I had to ask.'

It seemed logical to head back to the hospital until he could come up with a new plan but, as Dom turned a corner, he caught a glimpse of a view between the tall sides of central city buildings. The kind of view you could get from the roof of Seattle General with a glimpse of the waters of Elliot Bay in front of the impressive range of the Olympic mountains. The snow-capped peaks were reflecting this morning's sunshine as if they were lit from within.

It made Dom remember taking Emilia up to the hospital roof to have that very private conversation.

It also made him remember what she'd told

him that day they went jogging together in Discovery Park.

'That over there...' She'd been pointing at those very peaks. *'That's the Olympic National Park. If you want to clear your head and put your world to rights properly, then that's the place to go... It's my absolute favourite place in the world...'*

She'd said something else, too. About how long it took to get there. Hours to drive, even if you took a ferry to cut off some of the road distance.

He took his phone out and, by the time he was back at Seattle General, he had sourced what he needed. An elite private helicopter service which promised discretion along with meeting every need of their clients. Dom had never blatantly wielded either his wealth or his royal status but this was a situation he'd never found himself in before.

And it was more than urgent now. It was beginning to feel almost a matter of life or death.

How lucky was she?

Emilia stopped and raised her face to the winter sunshine as she took in the spectacular view surrounding her. She'd had to walk further than usual to get to this trail because the road was partially closed and she'd been worried when she'd gone to sign in at the Visitors' Centre that the trails might be closed as well but she'd been lucky. Not only were they open but, because it was the day before Christmas, it was unlikely there would be many other people out hiking.

So here she was, on her way to the top of this hill, feeling like the luckiest person on earth, as she took deep breaths of the icy, clean air, gazing across a snow-covered meadow at a forest of fir trees whose branches were drooping under the weight of snow. Beyond the forest, rocky snow-capped mountain peaks made a jagged horizon against the brightest blue sky Emilia had ever seen. She wanted to capture this moment for ever.

No…

What she really wanted was to share it. Because that's what made moments like this truly perfect, wasn't it?

And it had to be the right person. Someone who could understand how something like this could make you feel. How the sheer beauty of nature and the privilege of being able to become a part of it like this was enough to give you a huge lump in your throat and bring tears to the back of your eyes.

Someone who could make almost anything so much more meaningful. Who could share the thrill of facing what could seem an almost impossible medical challenge, like securing the airway and breathing of that man who'd fallen off the roof, and then share that blissful moment of success. Of knowing that you'd won. That you had the best job in the world and this was what mattered the most. *This* was who you were...

Yeah...someone who made the best moments even better.

But someone who made the not so good moments okay as well. Like when you did something stupid like cooking a turkey with the plastic bag still inside it. Or made your nervousness evaporate instantly with just a few words like, *'Trust me, Emmy... I've got this...'*

The picture-postcard scene of the mountains was blurring in front of her eyes and, to her astonishment, Emilia could feel her eyes overflowing. She actually had tears trickling down her cheeks for the first time since she had been a very young child.

Because she knew that it wasn't just 'someone' that she needed.

It was one person.

The man she would love for ever, even if it was impossible for them to be together.

Dom...

The squeeze in her chest was so painful that Emilia opened her mouth to cry out into the profound silence of the mountains but, as she did so, she became aware of another sound. A distant, rapid thumping that was getting steadily louder as it got closer.

'Wow...'

'Impressive, isn't it?' The pilot's voice was loud in Dom's ears through the headphones. 'Bit of a treat to get over here at this time of year.'

'Do you know the Olympic National Park well?'

'Sure do. Grew up in these parts and I've hiked every trail. Love the Grey Wolf Deer Loop and the Klahhane Ridge. Look...that's Steeple Rock down on our left. You can see where it got its name from, can't you?'

'Mmm…' The tall rock pillar was certainly distinctive. 'What's the building coming up?'

'The Hurricane Ridge Visitor Centre. I reckon your friend will have picked the Hurricane Hill trail. It's got everything you want on a day like this. Forest walks, snow, a good climb and the best view ever from the top of the hill.'

'And there'll be a place to land? Even if there's snow?'

'No worries. You might have to walk a bit. Can't land too close to trees.'

'I'll walk as far as I need to.'

The pilot grinned at Dom. 'Does she know you're coming?'

'How do you know it's a "she"?'

His grin widened. 'Just a hunch.'

Dom turned to stare down at the ground beneath them. 'This park is massive. I just hope we can find her.'

'If she's not in the forest, it won't be hard. You'll see…people stand out against snow.'

Especially when they were wearing bright colours like the solitary figure standing on a ridge. A bright red anorak that was the same shade as that gorgeous ballgown had been. A shade of red that was going to be Dom's favourite colour for the rest of his life.

'Looks like this might be where you need to be, mate.'

'Oh, yeah...' Dom kept his gaze locked onto that small patch of red, even when it almost vanished behind flakes of snow stirred up by the rotors. He didn't want to let Emilia out of his sight, for even a heartbeat.

She knew who it was, of course.

Getting dropped off by a helicopter into a remote wilderness area was something only somebody like a superstar or a prince would think of doing, wasn't it?

But that was irrelevant.

Because Emilia couldn't see a superstar or a prince walking towards her from the other side of this meadow as the helicopter took off again. She could just see a man. The man who, until very recently, she had known only as a colleague and rival—a person as ordinary as herself. And that was the man she had fallen in love with. That she'd been waiting for the chance to fall in love with for more than ten years...

She couldn't wait any longer.

It was pretty much impossible to run in snow shoes but Emilia gave it a shot. So did Dom. They almost made it but somehow both managed to lose their balance at the same time, falling into the cushion of soft snow but close enough that it took only a roll to be in each other's arms.

To hold. And be held.

To take turns to murmur, 'I love you…', 'I love you, too…' and 'So, so much…'

And to kiss…

Dear Lord…had anybody ever kissed like this? For this long? The heat of Dom's mouth and tongue was only increasing as the rest of Emilia's skin grew steadily colder but it wasn't until she shivered that Dom finally pulled back.

'You're cold… Here…take my coat…'

'Don't be daft. You need that yourself. We just need to start moving, that's all.'

'Where to?' Dom was smiling as he pulled Emilia to her feet.

'There's a great view from the top of this hill.'

They eyed each other. They could turn this into a competition to see who could go the fastest in snow shoes with the blink of an eye.

Emilia was up for it. She knew she would win so she gave Dom what she hoped was an inviting smile.

But he just laughed. 'I like the view I've got right now,' he said, bending his head to kiss her again.

'Mmm…' Emilia had to catch her breath when he released her. 'We could go home but it's a long drive. Do you need to call your helicopter to come back?'

'Why would I do that when that would mean you'd be driving back alone?' He held Emilia's chin in his hands. 'If I had my wish, it's that you would never be alone ever again. That I will always be with you.'

'You will…' Emilia had to blink back new tears. 'Even when you're not with me, you'll be in here…' She touched her gloved hand to her chest, over her heart, in a gesture she had learned from Dom. 'Always…but…'

A crease appeared between Dom's eyes. '…but?'

'But you have important things you need to do. Family things…'

'Ah…' Dom nodded. 'Family. *Sì*…that is something I need to talk to you about, *mio amore*.'

By tacit consent, they started walking. Back down the hill towards the road.

'You were right,' Dom told her.

'I always am,' Emilia murmured as she threw a grin in his direction. 'What about this time?'

'You said that family is everything.'

Emilia swallowed. Hard. Her heart skipped a beat but she wasn't going to buy into a fear that Dom was about to tell her he had to leave her to be with his family. She could feel the warmth of his touch, even through the thick wool of their gloves. She could hear the sincerity in his voice and she could see nothing but pure love in those beautiful, dark eyes.

'I want you to be part of my family.' Dom pulled Emilia to a halt again. 'I want us to create a family of our very own but…most of all… I just want to be with you. For the rest of my life. I want us to challenge each other like we always have so that we can always be our best in whatever we do. I want to dance with you. And make love with you…'

He kissed her again and Emilia's heart felt like it could split into a million pieces with how tender that kiss was. She wanted to tell him she felt exactly the same way but he wasn't finished yet.

'I used to think that being a doctor would be all I needed to be true to myself,' he told her softly. 'To be the person I always dreamed of being but that's not true now. Because I know I could never be everything I could be if I don't have you in my life.' His face was serious now. 'I know it won't be easy for you to make such big changes in your life but… we have a wonderful new hospital in Isola Verde so you could still work. And tell me about it every day when you come home. I'll be waiting for you if you'll let me. Marry me, Emmy…please?'

There were so many things Emilia wanted to say to Dom but there would be time for that later. So much time. The rest of their lives kind of time. For now, there was really only one thing she wanted to say. That she had to say.

'*Yes…*' Her throat was closing up as joy created more tears but she hadn't said *quite* enough yet.

'Yes, yes…*yes…*'

* * * * *

Look out for the next story in the
Royal Christmas at Seattle General quartet

Neurosurgeon's Christmas to Remember
by Traci Douglass

And there are two more festive
stories to come
Available December 2020!

If you enjoyed this story, check out these
other great reads from Alison Roberts

The Paramedic's Unexpected Hero
Saved by Their Miracle Baby
Awakening the Shy Nurse

All available now!